# Unwritten Path

## JOURNEY OF LOVE CHANGE AND SELF DISCOVERY

## KUNAL PARASWANI

# Contents

# THROUGH THE TUNNEL

Ramona and Elle stepped onto the metro at Victoria Terminal. The station was busy with the last commuters of the day, and their quick footsteps faded as the train doors closed.

Ramona breathed out sharply, showing her frustration.

"It's almost midnight," she said. "And for what? A meeting where decisions are already made. We're just there to agree and carry out their plans. What happened to value our input?"

Elle adjusted her bag and looked tired but thoughtful. "I know it feels chaotic," she said, biting her lip. "But I wonder... what if we give it time? Change can be messy, right? Maybe this new Company's Management will work if we just—" She stopped when she saw the sharp look in Ramona's eyes.

"It's exhausting," Elle said carefully. "But do you think we are being too hard on the Company's

Management? Maybe things will improve with the new CEO?"

Ramona held onto the cold metal pole, feeling its hardness. The train echoed in the tunnels, reminding her that time had passed quickly.

Ramona scoffed and spoke firmly. "Settle? Elle, this isn't just a phase; it's a situation. We worked together when the old CEO (his father) was in charge. Now, it's all chaos." She paused and looked away. "It's like they've forgotten we are people, not spare parts; they can just plug them into their new system."

Elle smiled slightly, but it didn't light up her eyes. "I understand. It's just..." Her voice faded as the train moved forward. "I don't know, Ramona. Maybe I'm too tired to think clearly."

The train moved through the city's underground. The carriage smelled grease and old leather, a reminder of the many people who traveled here daily. The fluorescent light flickered, creating shadows that matched their unease.

After a few stops, Elle glanced at her watch.

"This is me," she said softly as the automated voice announced her stop. Elle paused at the door, looking at Ramona. "Don't let it get to you," she said, her voice gentle but firm.

Ramona felt her friend's absence like a cold wind as the door closed. It made her feel smaller and more alone. Ramona managed a faint smile. "You too, Elle," she murmured, though her friend was already gone.

Ramona sat by the window and looked at her reflection. She saw a woman who once wanted to make a difference. Was she naive to think she could succeed in the corporate world? Each day made her care less and less. She felt a growing disillusionment and a deepening void within her, starkly contrasting with the vibrant, hopeful woman she used to be.

As the train moved quickly through the tunnels, she wondered if she could regain control. Could she stop being a part of their system and find meaning in her life again?

* * *

## Loneliness And Nostalgia

Ramona's phone buzzed in her pocket. Pulling it out, she saw a notification from Instagram—a photo from her sister, Rachael.

The image showed Rachel with her husband and daughter on a sunny beach. The warm light made everything look nostalgic, from the shining waves to the sandcastle they built, topped with tiny shells. The three of them smiled happily, a moment of true joy.

*The caption read: "Reliving our old childhood days with Jim and Lancy. Miss you, sis."*

Ramona's thumb hovered over the screen. She felt a tightness in her chest as an ache grew inside her. The photo reminded her of lazy afternoons spent building sandcastles with Rachael. They raced the tide, their laughter echoing along the shore during endless summers. For a brief moment, the warmth of those memories surrounded her, offering comfort to her tired spirit. But the stark contrast between those carefree days and her current reality only deepened her sense of loss and regret.

*The rhythmic clattering of the train brought her back to the present. She looked at the screen, her faint smile fading as reality hit her like a heavyweight. How did we end up here? she thought. Rach, you're living a stable life with family and joy. And me? What am I doing? I feel empty, just tired, disillusioned with my chosen life.*

*She started typing a reply but couldn't find the right words. Her reflection looked back at her from the dark screen, blurry from the unexpected tears. She blinked quickly, trying not to let them fall. Not here. Not now. Her struggle to compose a response to convey her conflicting emotions mirrored the internal turmoil she was experiencing.*

She put her phone away and rested her head against the window. The city moved quickly outside, blurred and busy, just like her thoughts. Somewhere, the warmth of that sunny beach remained just out of reach. But for Ramona, it felt like she was lost in a maze, unable to find her way out.

* * *

## Arrival At Home

The door creaked open, and Ramona entered the dim apartment. The silence wrapped around her like a familiar blanket—comforting but heavy. Her roommate, Bella, was away on a trip, making the place unusually quiet. Even the soft sound of the refrigerator seemed louder without her.

"Hello, house," she said, trying to sound lighthearted. "It's just you and me tonight."

After her quick shower, she warmed up a plate of leftovers in the microwave. The microwave beeped softly, breaking the silence. She took her meal to the balcony, opened the sliding glass door, and entered the cool night air. The stars above looked like silver dots in a dark sky, shining brightly despite the city's noise below.

She settled into her favorite chair, which creaked under her weight but felt comfortable like an old friend. Although she promised herself to quit, she reached for the pack of cigarettes she kept in the drawer for such moments. She lit one, took a deep breath, and felt the familiar burn in her lungs before exhaling a slow stream of smoke. The smoke curled into the night and disappeared like her fading hopes.

Music played softly from her speakers—classic songs she loved. These songs used to feel full of life, but now they seemed just out of reach. She closed her eyes and let the sad tunes surround her like a delicate blanket, offering a moment of escape from the restlessness inside her.

Her mind drifted to Tom. She still felt his presence, like a ghost she couldn't ignore. She remembered his face, his eyes crinkled when he smiled, and the passion that showed when he played his guitar. She could almost hear his steady, warm voice as he comforted her during her mother's passing.

"There was a lot of hope in our relationship," she thought, tracing the rim of her glass with her fingers. The memory felt bitter but carried a sadness that wouldn't disappear. "But his struggles—both with himself and his dreams— became our struggles, and neither of us could handle the burden."

She stubbed out her cigarette when it burned to the filter and watched the glowing ember fade. The stars above sparkled, reminding her of how big the universe is. It made her feel both comforted and mocked by her loneliness.

* * *

## Reflection

She reached under her mattress for her journal, which she had titled "My Quest for Focus, Clarity, and Meaning." The worn cover felt comforting in her hands, a physical reminder of herself amidst the chaos. She opened it to a blank page, pressed her pen to the paper, and began to write:

*Rach's picture affected me more than I thought it would. I'm not jealous—I'm genuinely happy for her. But it reminds me of what I've lost. I believed I would have my life together by now— a family and a home. I thought Tom and I could build that together, or at least we could. Maybe I was just kidding myself.*

She stopped and tapped the pen on the page as her thoughts tangled. The city's distant noise rose and fell, filling the quiet like a soft wave.

*"It's hard to accept that some dreams don't come true. But what's worse is not knowing what dreams to pursue next. I'm tired of feeling stuck. I bury myself in work and nights out that leave me*

*feeling emptier than before. I want something real. Something that feels important."*

She leaned back and looked up at the stars. Their steady light brought her quiet comfort, reminding her of the vastness of time. She closed her journal with a soft sigh, feeling a heaviness in her chest, but her mind started to clear. She stretched to relieve the stiffness in her muscles, then stood up and looked towards the horizon. The city lights shimmered—a lively reminder that life keeps moving, even when she feels stuck.

Picking up her phone, she opened the messaging app and typed a reply to her sister:

*"Happy for you, Rach. Beautiful pic. Let's catch up soon. Miss you too."*

She hit send, set the phone aside, and leaned on the balcony railing. The cool night air filled her lungs. The breeze brought a faint promise, a hint of something she hadn't felt in a long time: resolve.

*Maybe I don't have the answers yet, she thought as she looked at the sparkling city. But I will find them - one step at a time.*

# WHISPERS OF THE LOST SELF

amona had a successful career as a data analyst. She achieved many vital goals and steadily grew in her profession. At the same time, her relationship with Tom was thriving. Tall, handsome, and caring, Tom worked hard to make a name for himself in the music industry.

But in recent years, everything changed. First, Ramona's mother passed away, leaving a significant gap in her life. Soon after, her relationship with Tom ended, adding to her emotional pain. Work became more stressful and uncertain. One challenge after another piled up, slowly eroding her confidence and outlook. The vibrant, determined woman she once was faded, buried beneath doubt and exhaustion.

Each day feels the same—work, sleep, and endless scrolling through social media. Ramona knows she isn't happy. She misses the passion and purpose that once drove her, and deep down, she longs for something more.

Bella saw Ramona in distress and felt worried. Their friendship grew over the years they lived together, filled with late-night talks, shared challenges, and respect for each other. Now in her mid-forties, Bella made a brave choice years ago to leave her stable job and pursue her love for travel. This decision worked out well, and she became a successful social influencer with a loyal audience. Bella's life shows the power of following what matters. She hopes this can help Ramona at her current crossroads.

One calm evening, Bella talked to Ramona. "I know things have been hard lately. Sometimes, we just need a little self-care to feel better. Let's start small. How about a short meditation in the morning, a quick walk in the park, or a few minutes of journaling before bed? I'm here to help you through this."

Ramona felt overwhelmed by her thoughts and unsure about her life. She wanted to find a way to feel normal again. Looking at Bella, she found comfort in her friend's sincere concern and steady hope. Ramona nodded and said, "I promise I'll try it."

Ramona wanted to find inner peace, so she tried meditation. She sat cross-legged with her eyes closed and focused on her breath. However, her mind was full of thoughts: work frustrations, scattered memories of Tom, and a long to-do list. Her breath became shallow, and her body tightened. After ten frustrating minutes, she opened her eyes and said, "Is this supposed to calm me down?"

Journaling became difficult. What started as a New Year's resolution turned into a chore. She was used to typing on her laptop, so writing by hand felt awkward. She looked at the blank page and didn't know where to start. "Why am I doing this?" she asked herself. "This is a waste of time."

Even though she felt frustrated, Ramona trusted Bella enough to keep trying. She understood that change takes time and effort. "One step at a time," she reminded herself, hoping these new practices would bring her the peace and clarity she needed.

"I tried meditating today," Ramona admitted to Bella, her voice soft. "It was harder than I thought. My mind kept racing, and I couldn't quiet it down."

"That's completely normal," Bella reassured her. "Just keep practicing, and you'll start to see progress. Remember, it's about the journey, not the destination. And with journaling, don't overthink it. Write whatever comes to mind, even if it feels silly." Bella's words of encouragement were like a guiding light in the darkness of Ramona's uncertainty, giving her the strength to continue her journey of self-discovery.

Ramona sighed, her hope fading into doubt. "Okay, I'll try again tomorrow," she said quietly.

The next day, Ramona decided to go for a walk. The morning light filtered through the blinds, signaling it was time to embrace the day. However, instead of getting up, she lingered in bed, repeatedly hitting the snooze button. Eventually, the alarm fell silent, and she realized that her inaction weighed her down.

Feeling low as procrastination took over, Ramona sought refuge in a club that evening. There, she ordered a drink, claiming the moment as her own and allowing herself a brief escape from reality.

The music in the club softened, giving a brief break from the strong beats. Ramona sat at the bar with her fingers moving along the rim of her glass as her thoughts raced. She looked around, hoping to find distraction in the crowd of strangers.

Then, she noticed her.

A young woman sat alone at a small table near the stage. She was bent over a notebook, writing with intent. Occasionally, she paused to tap her pen against her lips as she thought. The warm light above her highlighted her focused expression.

Ramona unable to avert her gaze.

The woman was passionate about writing, wholly absorbed in her world. Her energy filled the air with a quiet joy, and at that moment, clarity struck.

Ramona felt a tightness in her chest. She realized what she was missing: enthusiasm, focus, and a sense of purpose. She used to have it. Nights spent scribbling ideas, her mind alive with stories and dreams—those memories now felt like a distant echo. Somewhere along the way, she had let it slip through her fingers. But in that moment, as she watched the young woman lost in her writing, a spark of recognition ignited within her. She realized that the vibrant, determined version of herself was not lost, just buried beneath doubt and exhaustion.

She glanced down at her drink, the faint reflection in the amber liquid staring back at her. She barely recognized the woman in the glass. The vibrant, determined version of herself felt like a stranger, buried beneath doubt and exhaustion.

Her gaze returned to the young woman, who smiled as if she had just discovered something new. Ramona felt a deep ache, not from envy but from longing. She longed for the energy she saw in the young woman and the passion it stirred.

She thought, 'I miss that part of myself,' feeling a surge of determination. She is still there—I just need to find her again.

Straightening in her seat, Ramona took a deep breath, her resolve hardening. Change wouldn't be easy, but she wasn't ready to give up on herself. Not yet.

As the band launched into a lively tune, she whispered, "I won't let this defeat me."

Ramona quietly promised to strive for a deeper understanding of herself, embrace transformation, and reignite her passion.

# THROUGH SHADOWS AND SUNLIGHT

The following day, Ramona woke up earlier than usual. Her body still felt tired from a restless night. She pulled back the curtains and saw the pale light of dawn breaking through the city skyline. The soft glow suggested a calm start to the day and a brief chance for peace. Rolling her shoulders, she took a deep breath, trying to let go of her heavy thoughts. As she prepared for her day, she told herself that today would be different.

Ramona remembered Bella's words: "There's a beautiful 4-kilometer trail not far from our place. You'll love it. Just give it a try." Ramona had nodded when Bella suggested it, but she felt doubt inside. She had always told herself that exercise wasn't for her. This morning, however, something changed. Maybe it was the hope of breaking free from her sadness or the wish not to let Bella down. Bella always believed in her potential.

Ramona laced up her sneakers and zipped her jacket tight against the chill. She looked in the mirror and met the gaze of a determined woman staring back at her. A spark of curiosity ignited in her eyes—something she hadn't experienced in ages. "I'm going to do this," she declared confidently, her voice resonating with resolve.

As Ramona stepped outside, the city felt different. The early light made it look calm. High-rise buildings shimmered in the soft dawn, their reflections moving on the glass while the streets were empty. This peacefulness felt like an invitation, encouraging her to move forward.

The trail unfolded like a serene painting. Towering trees swayed gently in the breeze, sunlight danced through the leaves, and a babbling creek added a soothing soundtrack. This natural beauty should have calmed Ramona, but her mind was still a storm.

A young couple jogged ahead, their laughter ringing out as they enjoyed each other's company. Ramona halted at the sight of them, unable to look away. Their vibrant energy stirred something deep within her, demanding her attention.

The memory came back clearly: Tom smiled at her, his hand brushing against hers as they ran to the park gate. They would fall onto the grass, laughing and out of breath, their faces red from running and joy. Those mornings belonged to them—a time she had taken for granted. Now, remembering that time felt painful, like a fresh wound.

Guilt grew in her chest. She had not put enough value on those moments—or Tom. He had tried to hold on, but she had focused too much on deadlines and her goals. She thought she had time, but time slipped away. Now, she was burdened by regrets and haunted by memories of what could have been. Her jaw tightened with bitterness. "Good for them," she said quietly, her words sharp and empty. She walked faster as if trying to escape her memories.

As she turned a corner, a sudden movement caught her eye. A squirrel darted across the path and swiftly scaled a tall oak tree. It paused midway, its fluffy tail flicking playfully. Ramona found herself smiling and even letting out a small laugh, which surprised her.

She paused momentarily, watching as the squirrel ran into the branches. Its endless energy was strangely comforting. And it broke through her bitterness since stepping onto the trail.

She felt some relief in her chest and took a deeper breath. She kept walking, and her pace became steadier. With each step, she noticed the harmony around her: the rustling leaves, the chirping birds, and the sunlight filtering through the trees. It was as if nature showed her life's quiet beauty—simple and humble, often overlooked in the rush of ambition and regret.

A memory of her mother surfaced. As a child, her mother would take her and Rachael on long walks, pointing out plants and birds and teaching them to appreciate the little wonders of the world. Tears filled her eyes, a bittersweet mix of sadness and gratitude.

At a bend in the trail, sunlight broke through the trees, creating a warm glow mixed with the shadows. The light and dark reminded Ramona of life's differences—how ambition can sometimes overshadow joy and how quiet moments can bring understanding. These thoughts didn't solve her problems, but they gave her a new way to look at things: maybe peace isn't something you have to chase; maybe it's something you let yourself feel.

*When she returned home, her shoulders felt noticeably lighter. The day stretched before her like a blank canvas, waiting to be filled. For the first time in weeks, she felt ready to face it. A hopeful thought emerged: Maybe today could be different.*

* * *

## Later That Day

Her phone buzzed. It was her sister, Rachael, calling from their hometown.

"Ramona!" Rachael said happily. "I have great news! Our investment is doing well and is providing us with amazing returns. There are also some legal formalities we need to address. Why not come for a visit? It's been a long time since you were last here."

"Really? That's great, Rachael!" Ramona sounded surprised and happy but felt a little sad, too. "I will come soon. I promise."

"And Lancy can't wait to see you!" Rachael added warmly. "She wants to show you the dollhouse she has for the doll you gave her."

Ramona smiled at the thought of her niece, feeling warmth in her chest. "I can't wait to see her and her dollhouse! Please tell her I'll be there soon."

Ramona put her phone down as the call ended, feeling an unexpected lightness. Her sister's comforting voice and the thought of her niece made her feel whole again after a long time.

As she approached her window, she looked at the busy city below. The noise of horns and chatter felt softer, almost inviting. Without hesitation, she grabbed her coat and decided to treat herself to a small celebration—visiting her favorite café.

* * *

## A Moment of Kindness

The cab rolled down the street when Ramona noticed the old gates of an orphanage she had seen many times before. She had always felt curious about it, but life often moved too fast for her to stop. Today, however, something felt different—like a soft pull at her heart.

"Could you please stop here for a moment?" she asked the driver.

*Ramona stood at the entrance of the Orphanage, feeling uncertain. The bright mural on the wall—a sun smiling down on stick-figure children—made her doubts feel even more substantial. She wondered, "Is this going to help? Am I just doing this to escape my problems?"*

Ramona pushed open the gate and stepped inside the orphanage. It was lively with activity. A Sister in a white habit greeted her with a calm smile. She heard children laughing from a nearby play area, which helped ease some of her tension.

"Hello, Sister," Ramona said calmly, though emotions swirled inside her. "I want to donate. It's not a lot, but I hope it can help."

The Sister smiled with gratitude. "That's a kind gesture, my child. Every donation, big or small, gives hope to these children. You're making a difference."

As the Sister walked with her through the grounds, Ramona saw children playing with a ball, their faces filled with joy. In another area, a small group gathered with crayons and paper, creating colorful drawings.

One child caught her eye—a girl with braided hair and a tattered dress who looked up from her drawing and waved at Ramona. Ramona waved back, her heart swelling with happiness.

She felt grounded for the first time in a long while—not by looking for answers or trying to escape, but by simply being present. The joy coming from the children reminded her of something she hadn't felt in ages: the deep fulfillment of giving and being part of something bigger than herself.

As she left the orphanage, her weight didn't disappear, but it felt lighter as if the joy she had witnessed had balanced it.

* * *

## Reflection and Gratitude

That evening, Ramona returned to her apartment and welcomed the quiet. She settled into her comfortable armchair, listening to the city hum outside as her thoughts flowed. Today had been a day of small victories: a walk that calmed her racing mind, a meaningful chat with her sister, and the bravery to visit the orphanage. These achievements weren't grand, but they felt significant.

She looked out the window at the city lights, twinkling like distant stars. Her mind drifted back to the couple she had seen on the trail that morning. Their laughter raised a question for her: Am I moving forward, or am I just going in circles?

Self-doubt crept in, whispering, "You'll never truly change.

"But another voice inside her, quieter but stronger, replied, "You can change. It's not about being perfect. It's about freeing yourself from doubt, one small step at a time. Keep trying, even when it's hard."

She leaned against the cool window glass and saw her reflection. Memories of her niece, the laughter of the children at the orphanage, and the warm sunlight through the trees played in her mind. These brief moments were important reminders of what mattered: connection, kindness, and the promise of growth.

Ramona took a deep breath and smiled gently. Though her journey was far from over, filled with uncertainties and unanswered questions, she had made significant strides today. That alone was enough to comfort her.

As the city pulsed around her, alive with energy, Ramona felt a quiet hope grow in her chest. It softly urged her on: Keep going. You're doing enough.

# BREATHING THROUGH THE CHAOS

R amona woke up to the warm sunlight streaming into her room. The morning felt calm and reminded her to enjoy the moment. She stretched, drank water, and moved to her favorite spot by the east window. Below, the city was waking up, with tall buildings visible against the bright dawn colors. She watched the new day begin and felt the sun's rays energize the skyline and soften the cool morning air. The warm light surrounded her, and for a brief moment, everything felt peaceful.

Birds sang outside, adding cheerful sounds to the quiet. Ramona took a slow sip of water, enjoying its coolness and calmness. These early moments felt special, connecting to a new day free from yesterday's worries.

The peace was interrupted by her alarm ringing, reminding her to meditate. She hesitated, not wanting to leave the calm that surrounded her.

After a short sigh, she got ready and paused in front of the mirror. Her tired reflection looked back at her, but she formed a small smile, a tiny sign of hope amid her worries.

Back in her room, she arranged a cushion on the floor to create a space for meditation. She sat down, crossing her legs and adjusting her position until it felt right. She closed her eyes and focused inward. At first, her breathing was uneven. She didn't fight it. Instead, she observed her breath with quiet curiosity.

Her restless mind brought up memories and fears. She acknowledged each thought without holding on to it or pushing it away. She let each thought float by like leaves on water. Whenever her mind drifted, she gently guided herself back to her breath.

As she meditated, her breath began to calm. It changed from shallow and erratic to a steady rhythm. She noticed tears running down her cheeks. These tears carried her sorrow and tension. Although they held some sadness, letting them flow made her feel exposed yet light. Sunlight streamed through the window, catching her tears and turning them into bright symbols of her healing journey.

She finished her meditation with a soft prayer of thanks, bowing her head until it touched the floor. It felt grounding and connected her to something more significant. When she stood up, she moved slowly, her heart feeling lighter and more at peace. She felt grateful for this moment, the peace it brought, and the strength it gave her.

Her smile returned, this time genuine and serene, without expectations—just pure acceptance. "Thank you, Bella," she whispered, grateful for guiding her to this peaceful place, showing the healing power of small habits and the strength that comes from new beginnings.

* * *

## Office affair

Ramona walked into the office feeling calm and smiling at her team as she headed to her organized office. After nearly ten years, she moved up from a junior analyst to head of the IT department. Her hard work and skills earned her the respect of her colleagues and management, making her a key player in company decisions. She had also built strong relationships with clients and suppliers, making her essential to the organization.

However, she often thought about leaving. The new management was changing the company culture in a way that made her uncomfortable. What was once a supportive and friendly environment was now focused mainly on profits.

Despite her dissatisfaction, Ramona found it difficult to leave her job, unsure of what lay ahead. Doubts lingered beneath her calm exterior.

As she checked her morning emails, one message stood out. It had the notes from the previous evening's management meeting, which included a task for her: to identify team members for layoffs as part of cost-cutting. The weight of this task added to her emotional turmoil.

She felt nostalgic thinking about the previous management. They had supported her during tough times, fostering loyalty and helping the team succeed. Everyone felt valued back then, creating a strong company culture. Now, that sense of community seemed lost. The focus on profits was weakening the bonds developed over the years.

Ramona leaned back in her chair and closed her eyes, recalling how she had once felt important in the company. She had a sense of purpose and belonging, but now the workplace felt unwelcoming.

Refusing to give in to despair, Ramona confronted the challenges ahead. She texted Elle, her trusted colleague, asking her to join for a coffee break.

Elle arrived quickly, bringing coffee with her. "Hey, Ramona," she said, settling into a chair across her.

Feeling relieved by Elle's presence, Ramona replied, "Thanks for coming by. I needed to talk."

"Of course," said Elle, sipping her coffee. "What's up?"

Ramona paused before speaking. "It's about that email regarding the layoffs. I can't stop thinking about it."

Elle sighed, her expression reflecting Ramona's unease. "I suspected as much. The word has already spread, somehow. The team is anxious, and a few are even discreetly exploring other opportunities."

Ramona felt heavy in her chest. "I can't believe this is happening."

"I know," Elle said gently. "But remember, it's not over yet. Let's take it step by step."

Ramona managed a small smile and felt a little better. "What would I do without you, Elle? Thank you."

Elle smiled back. "We'll get through this together, Ramona. Just like always."

Their chat ended when Elle's phone buzzed. "Oh, it's time for our team meeting! I need to finish my slides." She waved goodbye and returned to her desk.

The team discussed a significant drop in user engagement during the checkout process in the meeting. Ramona felt uplifted by their creativity and teamwork as they brainstormed ideas and solutions. For a moment, she remembered the passion that used to be part of the company culture.

The afternoon passed with various tasks: analyzing data to identify trends, aligning strategies with other departments, and turning complex metrics into clear team plans. Ramona found comfort in her work, knowing she was helping shape the company's future.

She reviewed her to-do list for the next week and reflected on her team's achievements. Even amid the uncertainty, she felt a spark of hope. She shut down her computer, took a deep breath, and prepared to leave the office, still unsure but determined to face what lay ahead.

* * *

## Journalling

Ramona curled up in her favorite chair on the balcony, a soft throw over her legs. The city lights twinkled below like stars, blending into the soothing sounds of distant traffic and gentle breezes. Her journal rested on her lap, reminding her of the promise she made to herself at the start of the year. What once felt like a chore now felt essential, a lifeline in the changes of her life.

Bella's gentle encouragement sparked her motivation, but Ramona's determination to find her true self kept her writing. She opened the Journal and smoothed her hand over the blank page, inviting her thoughts. After a moment's pause, she picked up her pen and began to write.

**"I woke up early today—something I haven't done in years. Watching the sunrise felt special. The sky changed colors—gold, rose, and lavender—offering hope and renewal. For a while, I just sat there, enjoying the peace. It felt like morning was saying, 'You can start over.'

I meditated longer than usual. I didn't mean to, but my body didn't want to move, and my heart wanted to stay calm. At one point, tears came—unexpected but cleansing. Sorrow and relief mixed, and I let them flow. I felt a part of me, buried under years of stress and doubt, finally coming to the surface. I hope I'm doing this right. For the first time in ages, I felt lighter.

Work had its usual problems, but things felt different. An email that would have stressed me out—a challenging message from management—didn't bother me today. I took a deep breath and responded calmly. It's a small step, but for me, it's big. I chose peace instead of panic. I decided not to let anyone else control how I felt. That feels like progress.

I couldn't get through this without Elle. She's my support, reminding me I'm not alone. Today, I made sure to tell her how much I appreciate her. Her smile when I said it meant everything. Gratitude does make things lighter.

As the day ended, I noticed something unusual—a feeling of cheerfulness. It's been so long since I felt that. Maybe it's the sunrise, the meditation, or Bella's wise words in my mind, but I'm grateful.

I am grateful for the sunrise, which reminded me of new beginnings. I am thankful for Bella's guidance, which helped me find myself again. I am pleased for Elle, whose kindness keeps me steady. These small joys feel like stepping stones on a path I'd forgotten.

Tomorrow, I'll remember the morning's peace. I'll focus on staying calm, no matter what challenges come up. I'll remind myself that I can control how I respond and protect my energy.

I'll hold on to Bella's words: 'Inner peace begins when you choose not to let someone else or a situation control your feelings.' This will guide me moving forward."**

Ramona set her pen down, feeling lighter than when she started. She closed the journal and placed it on the small table beside her. Reflecting felt like watering a thirsty plant—small but life-giving.

She leaned back, looking at the city skyline. The cool night air brushed against her skin, carrying the faint scent of jasmine from the neighbor's garden. The day's chaos seemed to fade away in the evening quiet.

Later, as she got ready for bed, she felt a rare sense of contentment. The world's weight hadn't disappeared, but it felt more manageable. A glimmer of peace settled within her for the first time in a long while—a soft, steady light to guide her forward.

# THE PATH FORWARD

Ramona's journey into meditation was no longer just a habit—it had become her lifeline. Over the months, her commitment deepened, and profound, almost imperceptible shifts came with it. What had once been clumsy, fleeting attempts to silence her restless mind transformed into an hour-long sanctuary—a ritual that left her grounded yet uplifted.

In her practice, Ramona often entered a space where the noise of her thoughts softened into a gentle hum, like a river easing into still waters. She felt a profound, unshakable peace in those rare, precious quiet moments. Once, as she focused on the steady rhythm of her breath and the point between her eyebrows, she became aware of a curious sensation—a warm, soothing current pooling there, as if her body were tenderly mending itself. The thought struck her like a whisper: her body, this remarkable vessel, had endured years of neglect yet remained faithful, patiently waiting for her to acknowledge and honor it.

Distractions still intruded, as they always would. But instead of resisting, Ramona let them drift past like clouds across an open sky—a skill she was slowly learning to extend beyond the mat. The practice wasn't always graceful, especially on days when emotions surged, dragging her into deep wells of reflection. Yet, Ramona reminded herself that transformation wasn't a dramatic leap but a steady, deliberate walk—one mindful step at a time.

The changes rippled outward in unexpected ways. The qualities Ramona once thought buried—patience, resilience, and quiet strength—began reappearing as constant companions. She noticed a change at work. Her newfound empathy significantly enhanced her communication skills. Conversations that once felt like mere business transactions evolved into genuine connections. She listened with the intent of understanding rather than simply responding.

In a meeting with a long-standing supplier, Ramona felt the tension in their voice. Delivery delays had strained the partnership and the weight of finding a resolution pressed on her. In the past, she might have responded defensively, guarding her position. Instead, she leaned into the moment, her calm demeanor disarming the room. "I understand your concerns," she said, her tone steady and sincere. "Let's explore a solution that works for both of us." It was a subtle shift, but the effect was unmistakable; she saw the supplier's stance soften, their guardedness giving way to collaboration.

Ramona's social life, too, began to shift in texture and meaning. A quiet, authentic kinship now replaced the superficial connections that once left her feeling hollow. She no longer sought validation through grand gestures or performative bonds—those fleeting displays that once seemed to define her worth but ultimately left her craving more. Instead, she began to find comfort in the most minor exchanges: a nod from a stranger on her morning walk, the warmth of a shared smile with a barista, or the rare honesty of a heartfelt conversation.

These simple moments carried a depth she hadn't thought possible, affirming a quiet truth she had overlooked for years—that connection didn't need to be loud to be authentic. In conversations where walls came down and words felt raw and unfiltered, Ramona discovered a warmth she hadn't known she longed for. These exchanges didn't demand anything from her beyond presence; in them, she found solace far richer than applause or admiration could ever provide.

For the first time in years, Ramona felt like she truly belonged. It wasn't because of what others thought of her or any big moment. A quiet, steady feeling grew inside her, just for herself. This internal assurance eased her relationships, allowing her to move through life with an authenticity that felt liberating and profoundly grounding.

* * *

At first, Ramona saw her morning walks as a duty, but now they have become a beloved part of her day. These quiet early hours help her find peace before the busy day starts. Her coworkers noticed her improved energy and complimented her, but the real reward was how good she felt inside. She walked lighter, stood taller, and smiled real.

As she walks, she discovers a new world around her. Instead of rushing through her neighborhood, she now enjoys the beauty in everyday things. The morning sun casts a golden glow on the old brick buildings, transforming them into something extraordinary. Wildflowers grow from cracks in the sidewalk, showing that beauty can thrive in surprising places. Birds sing beautiful songs in the morning as they welcome the day. Their sounds blend with the soft rustling of leaves in the wind.

Loneliness, once an unwelcome reminder, has taken on a different hue. Now, solitude was her serene companion. The quiet early hours provide her a sanctuary to unwind, ponder, and simply be.

Her walks also help her connect with her neighbors—an older man with a friendly golden retriever (dog ) waves at her daily. A mother with groceries and a stroller accepts her help with a thankful nod, and their brief chat creates a moment of shared understanding. Though seemingly inconsequential, these fleeting interactions wove themselves into the fabric of her mornings, adding a sense of connection she hadn't realized she was missing. They also bring a sense of joy and fulfillment, reminding her of the beauty of human connection.

Through these walks, Ramona has found joy in being present. Each step was a promise to herself to care for her well-being. She sees life as something to enjoy and explore instead of just a list of tasks to check off.

* * *

Journaling had become an essential part of Ramona's routine—a personal space where she could express her thoughts freely. Putting pen to paper was unexpectedly trans-formative, uncovering truths she had long buried beneath the chaos of her daily life. At first, her writing was slow and careful, but as she continued, she became more open and honest. The blank pages encouraged her to examine her thoughts, helping her untangle the overwhelming worries.

As Ramona wrote, she noticed that her mind often made minor problems seem much more significant than they were. Journaling allowed her to see how she exaggerated situations and let them control her feelings. She found that they lost their strength by writing down these overwhelming thoughts. This practice grounded her and provided a safe space to explore her fears, untangle her emotions, and turn her anxious thoughts into clear ideas and focus.

Through her journals, she found patterns in her behavior—habits of self-sabotage, fears she had hidden even from herself, and a strong need for control that often made her stressed. These realizations weren't always easy to face. Some days, she had to stop writing, with her pen hovering over the page, as she dealt with the weight of what she had uncovered. But even during these uncomfortable moments, Ramona felt strange freedom. The things that scared her started to feel smaller as she understood them better.

Journaling helped her develop self-compassion, which she had struggled to find. She began to see her mistakes not as failures but as part of being human—imperfect steps that supported her growth. Each journal entry became a conversation with herself, allowing her to understand rather than judge herself. Over time, she learned to treat her flaws and mistakes with the same kindness she would offer a friend, seeing them as stepping stones toward becoming the person she wanted to be.

Journaling was not just a habit for Ramona but a necessary tool. It reminded her that no matter how chaotic life became, she could always find a quiet and honest place within herself.

The journey had its challenges. Some nights, loneliness crept in quietly, bringing doubts that troubled Ramona's confidence. The urge to fall back on old habits—like distracting herself to avoid her feelings—was intense in those challenging moments. But Ramona started to build tools for herself, finding small ways to stay afloat when uncertainty hit hard. She relied on meditation, took morning walks, and journaling. These practices helped her return to the calm she was learning to create.

Her transformation didn't go unnoticed. Bella, her ever-supportive friend and confidante, had watched Ramona's subtle but significant changes with quiet admiration. One evening, as they sat together in the living room, sipping steaming cups of herbal tea, Bella's face lit up with a warm smile.

"I am very proud of you," Bella said with warmth. "The peace you've found is inspiring. You are changing, Ramona. There's a meditation retreat just outside the city that I think you would enjoy experiencing. Spending days in silence is tough but can be a powerful experience. The energy in the group sessions feels amazing."

Bella's words were like sunlight breaking through clouds, showing her how far she had come.

"That sounds great, Bella," Ramona said calmly. "Thank you. I'll look into it—maybe after I visit my sister. Work has been a lot, but this feels like something I need to do."

The conversation shifted to lighter topics, such as their favorite books, plans for the future, and shared memories. However, Ramona still felt a spark of anticipation. She was excited about the retreat and pushing herself in a new way.

# PROFESSIONAL GROWTH

Ramona's personal growth has dramatically changed her work life. She went from being easily distracted and making mistakes to becoming a focused, driven professional. This change has improved her productivity and efficiency, allowed her to explore new ideas, and made her a better leader.

Her colleagues noticed Ramona's positive change. Her calm and poised attitude helped the team during stressful times. She showed confidence, which encouraged others to face challenges with hope. Her increased patience and fresh perspective led to many new solutions that often exceeded expectations. As a result, she earned her peers' respect and her supervisors' trust. More importantly, her personal growth inspired her colleagues to strive for self-improvement, creating a more dynamic and productive team.

Ramona's relationship with the company's new management improved. What had been a source of frustration became a chance to work together. She realized that growth meant adapting and faced the changes with strength and an open mind.

She worked with Elle to minimize the number of layoffs in their department. While some cuts were necessary, they promoted a caring approach by offering voluntary resignation packages. This way, employees had options and could maintain their dignity during tough times.

Ramona and Elle's thoughtful leadership has been a game-changer. Their ability to balance the company's needs with genuine care for their colleagues has earned them respect and recognition as empathetic leaders. Their reputation for prioritizing their team's well-being reassures everyone they are in good hands.

Despite her successful career, Ramona was facing new challenges. In a recent meeting, tensions rose when the latest purchasing manager—Elle's fiancé—proposed switching the company's leading vendor. He argued that other vendors offered credit terms, while their current one required almost immediate cash payments. The company's auditor agreed, saying the change could be financially beneficial in the long run.

But Ramona pushed back. The company had tried this before and returned to its current vendor after facing delays and quality issues with the new one. Production had suffered, and so had the final product.

A heated debate followed, with different departments weighing in. In the end, Ramona's suggestion won out: They would place a small test order with the new vendor while keeping their existing supplier. Management appreciated her insight and acknowledged her experience and foresight.

Still, as people left the boardroom, whispers lingered—*It's always Ramona's way.*

* * *

## The Rise of Rumors

Rumors began to spread about Ramona, damaging Ramona's reputation. The team discussed an alleged inappropriate relationship between Ramona and Sam, the vendor's CEO. They accused her of favoritism because she had more influence in decisions and was selected to represent the company at an international conference. The fact that Ramona had helped Sam with his startup made the gossip seem more believable to those who doubted her.

Ramona was surprised by the sudden changes at work. She had always been proud of her honesty, so the accusations hurt her deeply. Her closest friend, Elle, chose to stay neutral. She was caught between her loyalty to Ramona and her connection to the purchasing manager, which left Ramona feeling lonely and hopeless.

At one point, Ramona considered quitting. She found it challenging to work in an environment of mistrust and hostility.

Instead of letting the situation overwhelm her, Ramona took control and faced the challenges head-on.

* * *

## Confrontation and Resolution

Ramona stayed composed and let the rumors fade on their own. Her coworkers' anger lessened over the next few days, but some still treated her coldly.

Ramona discovered that a small group of new hires known for causing drama started the gossip. Their efforts to turn others against her didn't succeed.

In a team meeting, Ramona addressed the rumors about her relationship with Mr. Sam. She firmly and confidently stated, "Let me set the record straight: my relationship with Mr. Sam is strictly professional. I make decisions based solely on what is best for this organization."

HR manager stood for Ramona's support. His response calmed the situation. "We are here to do our jobs, not to discuss rumors that hurt team spirit," the HR manager said. "If anyone has real concerns, please come to me directly."

The HR manager's intervention relieved Ramona and eased the tension in the room.

Exhausted from constant stress, Ramona decided to take a break. This vacation wasn't just time off—it was a chance to visit her sister, escape daily pressures, and clear her mind.

# BETWEEN STATION

Ramona was excited as she prepared for her journey back to her hometown. The prospect of a full day's journey by train, with its promise of scenic beauty, filled her with a sense of adventure. She carefully selected gifts for her loved ones and eagerly noted down the best places to visit and foods to try during her stay. She made a firm promise to herself to leave thoughts of work behind. With a novel in hand, she was ready to immerse herself in its story and escape the digital world.

In the quiet early morning, before the city was fully awake, Ramona arrived at the station. The sky was dark, and a chilly air hung around her as she boarded her train. She had chosen a window seat in the executive chair car, and sinking into her seat made her smile at her decision. The coach was calm, with only a few passengers already settled in, and the seat next to her was empty. Soon, the soft sound of the engine signaled their departure, and the train moved smoothly out of the station.

As the train rolled along, the rhythmic sound of the tracks soothed Ramona's senses. A steward appeared, offering her a steaming cup of tea. She cradled the warm cup, feeling the tension in her shoulders melt away. Beyond the window, the city gradually transformed into serene countryside. The early morning sun cast a golden glow on the lush fields, where buffaloes roamed freely. This peaceful scene mirrored the tranquility she sought during her journey.

Ramona looked out the window at the beautiful scene. The sky was wide open, the sun shone softly, and the peaceful countryside rolled by. At this moment, she felt the stress of her daily life fade away, and a sense of calm and contentment took its place. She slowly sipped her tea, enjoying the quiet escape she had been craving.

Her peaceful moment was abruptly interrupted by laughter from the seat beside her. She turned to see a family: a couple with their two young daughters giggling over a book. The girls' innocent joy stirred a wave of nostalgia in Ramona, returning her to her childhood. She remembered the carefree days of traveling with her parents and sister when their family felt perfect and whole. But life had changed. Her parents had divorced, and even though her father tried to stay connected, everything had shifted after he remarried. He made efforts to bridge the gap, calling, leaving messages, and attending their mother's funeral. But the bond between Ramona and her sister with their father had weakened, lost in the chaos of their lives.

She wondered if it was time to change that. She and her sister could plan a reunion, a chance to bridge the gap that had grown between them and their father. The idea filled her with hope.

Setting her cup down, Ramona picked up her novel and let the words carry her away. The train's rhythmic hum and the carriage's gentle sway lulled her into a peaceful state. Her tranquility was momentarily disrupted as the train made its next stop, bringing a new passenger into her carriage. An older man, perhaps in his sixties, entered with a quiet confidence. His face bore a peaceful glow as if he were content with life. He greeted the attendant with a polite nod before settling into the seat beside her.

As the train sped up, he looked at Ramona and broke the silence in a friendly way. "It's nice to see someone reading a book instead of looking at their phone. That seems rare these days."

Ramona looked up from her book, a soft smile spreading. "I guess I'm trying to escape screens whenever possible. I spend most of my day glued to one at work, so I like to disconnect when I have some free time."

He nodded firmly. "That's an excellent approach. Life has certainly become dominated by screens, hasn't it? By the way, I'm Henry."

She chuckled and said, "Nice to meet you, Henry. I'm Ramona."

"Likewise, Ramona. It's interesting to share this with you. Recently, I started volunteering with an NGO where I teach sketching to older adults and villagers. Many don't realize their smartphones can help them learn to draw, so we stick to traditional methods instead. They enjoy it! A few times a week, I make the trip to the community. I live on a small farm a few stations away."

Ramona smiled, feeling intrigued. "You're an artist at heart," she whispered.

Henry looked at the book she was holding. "I've read that novel before. It's a nice story that acts as a guide to a better life."

Ramona's eyes brightened. "Really? I've found it interesting so far."

He leaned in a bit and spoke as if sharing a secret. "The part where the main character learns to let go of control resonated with me. It was a reminder that sometimes life works best when you stop trying to force everything into place."

Ramona noticed a change in the atmosphere between them. "That's where I am," she said. "I'm learning to let go of things—people, expectations, and pain. It's not easy."

Henry nodded slowly and kept his eyes on hers. "It never is. Letting go feels like losing initially, but it opens up space for something new." He paused and added, "I'd like to share a metaphor with you if you are interested."

"Please, go ahead," she replied, curious."

Our connections in life resemble ripples in a pond when a stone is thrown. Each ripple embarks on its journey, occasionally intersecting with others. Sometimes, these intersections uplift us, while at other times, they can disrupt us at different times. The time we share may be brief or long-lasting, but ultimately, we all continue along our chosen paths.

They enjoyed the silence for a moment, both lost in their thoughts. Then, with a warm smile, Ramona said, "That's so beautiful! It reminds us to let go of the things we can't control."

As the train moved along, the warm light of the setting sun filled the coach, making the passengers glow. Henry looked out the window and saw familiar places that meant his station was close. He turned to Ramona and smiled softly.

"Looks like my stop is coming up," he said as he adjusted his backpack. "You will have a beautiful journey ahead. Don't miss the sunset over the sea."

Ramona looked at him, her eyes showing the fading light. "It's been nice talking to you, Henry. Thank you for everything."

Henry nodded at Ramona, his expression showing a bit of nostalgia. "I feel the same way, Ramona. Take care of yourself. Good luck with everything ahead."

The train began to slow down, and the brakes screeched loudly. Henry stood up and slung his bag over his shoulder. He hesitated as if there was more he wanted to say, then settled for a quick wave.

"Bye, Ramona," he said softly but sincerely.

"Bye, Henry," she replied, watching him walk towards the door. "Take care."

The train doors slid open with a hiss, and Henry stepped onto the platform. Ramona watched him for a moment, then turned back to the window. As the train started to move, she saw the sea in the distance, the sun setting on the horizon, painting the sky with a vibrant mix of orange and pink.

Ramona sat on the train, listening to its steady hum. She looked out at the beautiful landscape, filled with light and nature. For the first time in a long while, she felt both awe and a profound peace inside her, a tranquility that seemed to seep into her soul. Henry's words echoed in her mind, reminding her that letting go is not about losing but making space for something new. The connection, the moment, and the journey all felt unexpectedly perfect.

# FAMILY LIFE

Ramona stepped off the train and into the cool night air. She took a deep breath, enjoying the fresh air. A small smile appeared on her face. Though old and worn, the station felt lively and active. She heard quiet conversations, smelled tea from a nearby stall, and caught the distant sound of another train leaving.

She called for a cab, and as it drove through the quiet streets, the streetlights lit up the paths she knew well. These roads were not just a way to get to her destination; they were connected to her childhood memories and the essence of the place that shaped her. Her hometown was not just a physical location—it was a feeling, a safe space of familiarity and warmth.

The buildings she passed were more than just structures; they held memories from her childhood. Each one carried a piece of her life. The schoolyard, where she and Rachael chased each other and laughed, still stood with its slightly rusted gates. The corner cafe, where she spent weekends talking about dreams with her friends over steaming cups of tea, looked the same, with its faintly flickering neon sign. The quiet park, where she learned to ride a bike with her father's help, appeared in front of her, its trees swaying gently in the breeze as if waving hello.

It had been years since she left her hometown to pursue her career. Time had changed the town, making it cozier and more charming, but its core remained the same. Whenever she returned, it felt like putting on a favorite, well-worn coat that still fit perfectly. This familiarity gave her comfort and a sense of stability she missed in the bustling city life, a stark contrast to the tranquility of her hometown.

As the cab neared Rachael's house, she felt excited. The porch light shone softly, welcoming her home. Tonight, the house was more than just a building; it was a place for re connection, where memories would mix with future conversations. Ramona leaned back in her seat and enjoyed the moment. For the first time in a long while, she felt nostalgic and peaceful, as if she was exactly where she needed to be, a feeling of belonging washing over her.

The door opened before she could knock, and Rachael greeted her with a big smile. Behind her were Jim, Rachael's husband, and Lancy, their daughter, also smiling warmly.

"You're finally here," Rachael said, giving Ramona a tight hug. Her sister's warmth enveloped Ramona, offering comfort and a sense of belonging.

Stepping through the door, Ramona met with a wave of joy, conversation, and warmth. Rachael and Jim had fashioned a simple yet loving home with their daughter Lancy at its heart. The house exuded an understated elegance, adorned with handmade items, and carried a faint scent of freshly baked cookies, a testament to the warmth and love that filled the space.

Rachael, a homemaker, worked hard to create a warm and welcoming home. Jim, an auditor, brought his careful attention to detail and humor to their family life. But Lancy, their lively two-and-a-half-year-old, brought the house to life—her new ability to say a few words filled every conversation with joy and excitement.

When she proudly called Ramona "Aunt Ramona," it warmed Ramona's heart. Although this title surprised her, it felt meaningful—it connected her to a family she had admired from a distance but now felt part of. At that moment, Ramona realized how much she had longed for this sense of belonging.

As the evening went on, the tiny house filled with lively conversation. Rachael talked about her day, sharing funny stories about Lancy and updates about friends. Jim shared his thoughts about work and holiday plans, while Ramona told her own stories, describing her life in the city. With her innocent questions, Little Lancy added a touch of humor and thoughtfulness to the conversation.

"Why do stars twinkle, Aunt Ramona? Do they laugh like we do?" Lancy asked, her big eyes full of wonder.

"Maybe they do," Ramona said with a soft laugh, brushing hair from Lancy's face. "Or maybe they're winking at us, telling us to dream."

Lancy tried hard to stay awake but gradually lost the battle against sleep. Her parents found her struggle amusing. She snuggled closer to her mother, enjoying every word and laugh. In the end, sleep took over. Rachael gently picked her up, cradling her daughter's tiny head on her shoulder, feeling the calm weight of a sleeping child.

As they settled down for the night, the house became quiet, except for the occasional creak of the floorboards and the soft rustle of the wind against the windows. Rachael and Jim lay safely between them in their room with Lancy. They could feel her tiny chest rise and fall as she slept, her peaceful face lit by the moonlight coming through the curtains. The serenity of the night enveloped them. These moments represented the small successes of being parents—a reminder of everything they had built together.

In the guest room, Ramona lay awake, wrapped in a soft quilt that smelled of lavender. The room was simple but welcoming, with small details that showed Rachael's care—a small vase of fresh flowers by the window, a stack of books on the bedside table, and a light scent of eucalyptus from a reed diff-user. The ticking clock in the hallway marked the passing of time, reminding Ramona of the life happening within these walls.

She remembered earlier conversations, the laughter in the house, and the warmth of being with her family. But as her thoughts drifted, a slight ache appeared, a longing she couldn't name. Rachael's simple life and happy family contrasted sharply with her mixed-up life. She had chosen a different path—a city life filled with ambition and achievements. Yet now, in the quiet of the night, she wondered if she had given up something important for her success. The stark contrast between the two lifestyles created a tension she couldn't shake off.

Ramona remembered the warmth of the dining table where they shared love and connection. Their laughter and understanding filled the room with comfort. In contrast, dining alone felt cold and empty, missing the warmth she craved. This realization caused pain, and soon, tears streamed down her cheeks.

Wanting to distract herself, she left the bed and walked to the side table for water. Her footsteps echoed in the quiet room.

Her gaze landed on an old photo album on the side table, its corners slightly frayed. A wave of nostalgia washed over her as she picked it up and began to flip through its pages. The photos told a story of love, laughter, and togetherness: birthday parties with cakes and balloons, family outings under the bright sun, and school events where she and Rachael stood side by side, arms entwined.

One photo caught her eye—a picture of her and Rachael as children, their faces glowing with joy as they posed in front of a sandcastle they built during a summer vacation long ago. This image made her smile, but a touch of sadness accompanied it. That younger version of herself, filled with dreams and hopes, now felt like a stranger. Life had pulled her away from those carefree days. Although she had gained much, she couldn't shake the feeling that she had lost something important.

The rain softly tapped on the window, bringing her back to the moment. She closed the album and set it on the table, her fingers lingering on its cover.

In the stillness of the night, she made a silent vow to herself. This journey was significant. It was an opportunity to rekindle her bond with her family and with buried parts of herself. It was a chance to pause, release the constant pressure, and find joy in the enduring, simple love that surrounded her.

As sleep finally took her, Ramona felt a peace she hadn't felt in years.

The smell of fresh coffee and Lancy's laughter woke Ramona the following day. She stretched under the soft quilt and let the sunlight from the window help her wake up. The scent of toasted bread and butter mixed with the coffee pulled her out of bed.

In the kitchen, Rachael hummed a tune while she flipped pancakes. Jim sat at the table, helping Lancy pour juice into her bright cup. This heartwarming scene made Ramona smile, feeling the warmth of their family bond.

"Good morning, sleepyhead," Rachael teased as Ramona walked in. "Lancy has been asking why Aunt Ramona doesn't wake up as early as she does."

Ramona laughed and ruffled Lancy's hair as she sat down. "Because Aunt Ramona needs her beauty sleep to keep up with you, little one."Lancy giggled, her eyes sparkling. "But I wake up early, and I'm pretty, too!"

"You've got me there," Ramona replied, laughing.

They enjoyed breakfast together, and the warm atmosphere helped Ramona feel better after the heavy feelings she had the night before. Soon after, Jim left for work, leaving the women to enjoy a quiet day.

As the day went on, Ramona found solace in the simple joys of being home. She joined Rachael in the kitchen and fell into a nice rhythm. They chopped vegetables, kneaded dough, and shared stories as they worked. The comforting flow of cooking brought Ramona a profound sense of peace.

Nearby, Lancy played with her dollhouse, her laughter filling the room. She created a story with dolls, a talking dog, and a brave rescue mission where the dolls had to save their friend from a pretend danger. Occasionally, she would show Ramona a doll's outfit or ask for help with her story.

While they worked, the sisters shared their thoughts.

"It's great to see you settled, Rachael," Ramona said as she set down a tray of cookies to cool.

"Thanks to God, everything is going well," Rachael replied, smiling softly. She paused, her hands resting over a mixing bowl. "But sometimes, I miss my teaching job. Being a homemaker is fulfilling, but it can feel a bit dull. I've been contemplating returning to work once Lancy starts school." Rachael's inner conflict resonated with Ramona, making her feel more connected to her sister's journey.

Ramona leaned against the counter, deep in thought. "It's funny how we all feel unsatisfied with our lives. Watching you, I wonder what my struggles have been for. You have so much peace and love in your life. You should appreciate these moments."

Rachael tilted her head and searched Ramona's face. "Maybe you're right," she replied softly. "But you seem so calm and grounded these days. Is it because of those practices you mentioned? Or..." She hesitated, a teasing look in her eyes. "Is there someone new in your life?"

Ramona laughed and shook her head. "I can't even think about starting a new relationship right now."

"Well," Rachael said with a playful smile, "Jim still talks to Tom. Tom is doing well with his music career and often asks about you. Maybe it's time to see if you two can reconnect?"

Mentioning Tom brought back memories for Ramona, like the soft sound of a book being opened gently. Was she ready to revisit that past or start something new with him?

Her smile faded, and she quickly changed the subject. "Let's talk about those legal matters regarding our investments."

Rachael noticed a change but chose to ignore it. "Oh, we need to sign the new rental agreement for Mom's house. The property value has increased since the government announced a new project nearby. Our investments have also doubled. Jim thinks it's wise to book some of the profits."

Ramona smiled, looking happy. "That's great news. Let's get the paperwork done and book the profits."

"I'll call Jim and let him take care of it," Rachael said firmly.

Ramona thought momentarily and then said, "This feels like a reason to celebrate. Let's organize a family gathering at the beach club, just like we used to—with Dad there, too." She paused, tracing her finger around her coffee mug. "And maybe we could invite Nancy," she added quietly.

She hesitated, feeling the weight of her words. "I know we haven't been close to her since she married Dad," she said, looking at Rachael. "But I keep thinking... maybe it's time to change that. For years, Nancy has reminded us of things we didn't want to face—Dad moving on, the space Mom left behind, and the fear that letting her in would mean letting go of the past." Her voice shook slightly.

"But sitting here now, I wonder if holding on to those feelings is worth it. Maybe letting them go could bring us a real connection." The prospect of a new beginning with Nancy brought a hopeful light to the conversation.

Rachel leaned back, her expression thoughtful. "Nancy..." she said softly, her brow furrowing. After a pause, she nodded with a warm smile. You're right. She has always been kind, even when we didn't let her in. I think it's time we made an effort. Let's do it." Her reassurance was palpable, bringing a sense of comfort to the conversation.

# TIDES OF REUNION

J im was packing for the beach club trip, ensuring everything was ready. Meanwhile, Mr. George felt joy after getting an unexpected call from his daughter, Ramona. She invited him to a family gathering, which filled him with anticipation. He quickly promised her he and his wife would attend, his voice brimming with excitement.

After hanging up, George turned to his wife, Nancy, with a smile that radiated their deep love. "Ramona wants us to join them at the beach club," he said, sounding excited and nostalgic. "It's been so long since we've all gathered as a family. It'll be like the old days, but better."

Nancy smiled brightly, her eyes lighting up as she heard the news. "Oh, that's a great idea! I'm so happy the girls thought of this. It's time for us to reconnect." She hesitated, a hint of worry showing on her face. "But George, do you think I'll make things awkward? The girls don't know me as well as they know you. I don't want to ruin anything."

George moved closer and spoke softly but confidently. "Nancy, don't worry. Ramona reaching out is important. It shows they want this; they want us. If we don't go, it might look like we're holding back."

Nancy thought about his words and nodded slowly. "You're right," she said, smiling again. "Let's not waste time. We should find something special for Lancy and the others—a small gift to show we care."

As they started preparing for the gathering, they felt hope and excitement. This was a firm reminder that time had not weakened their connections but had allowed them to build even stronger ones.

Meanwhile, at Rachael's house, Jim finishes packing the last bags for the beach club trip. He felt slightly accomplished as he looked at the neatly arranged items. Across the room, Ramona sat on the couch, lost in thought. It had been months since she had seen her parents.

While Ramona felt excited about the reunion, she also felt a deep sense of anxiety. She worried about Nancy, her father's wife. Would Nancy feel welcome? Would old tensions resurface and make things uncomfortable?

Rachael noticed her sister's worried expression and walked over to her. She gently placed a hand on Ramona's shoulder. "Ramona," she said softly, "everything will be okay. Nancy wants to connect with us, too. This reunion is not just for them; it's for all of us. It's a good start."

Jim spoke up from across the room, his steady voice calming Ramona's worries. "It's just a day at the beach," he said, encouraging her. "Focus on having fun together. If we stay open-hearted, everything will work out. It always does."

Ramona took a deep breath, feeling a bit better. She nodded but still felt the weight of her concerns. She worried their efforts to improve their relationships might show how distant they were.

Lancy was excited, moving around the apartment and discussing everything she wanted to do at the beach club. Her happy energy lightened the mood. Busy with last-minute errands, Rachael checked her phone and called Jim, "I'll pick up the desserts and extra towels on my way back. Do we need anything else?"

As the time for family gathering approached, the apartment buzzed with anticipation and a touch of nerves. Each person held onto the hope that this day at the beach would be more than just a fun outing—it could be the catalyst for them to grow closer as a family.

The family arrived at the beach club in the afternoon. The sun shone brightly in the blue sky, warmed by a cool breeze that carried the salty smell of the sea. They could hear the gentle rustling of palm trees mixed with children's laughter and people talking. The sand was warm under their feet, and waves crashing on the shore added to the serene atmosphere. It was a great day for a picnic.

The club was bustling with activity. Colorful towels covered the sand, and groups of people gathered under large umbrellas or relaxed near the water. The sound of waves crashing on the shore blended with the happy noise of the crowd. Thanks to Jim's planning, they secured a tremendous prime spot on the patio's edge with a breathtaking ocean view.

As soon as they stepped onto the patio, Lancy tugged at Ramona's hand. She paused, her eyes wide with excitement as she entered the scene. "Beach!" she shouted happily, pointing to the waves. "Water!" Ramona couldn't help but smile at her niece's pure joy. Moments like these made all the planning and traveling worth it.

"Yes, sweetheart, that's the ocean," Ramona replied, kneeling to her level. "It's big, isn't it?"

"Big!" Lancy repeated, stretching her arms to measure the sea. Her curls bounced as she giggled, looking from the water to the sky and back.

Rachael crouched down beside her, smiling warmly. "What do you think, Lancy? Do you like it?"

Lancy turned to Rachael, her face full of wonder. "Like! Like!" she said, clapping her hands. Then she added, "Happy!"

Soon, George and Nancy arrived, bringing a lively energy to the gathering. George's loud laugh signaled their arrival before they approached the group, and Nancy's bright smile lit up the entire patio. Their presence added warmth and excitement, like finding the missing pieces of a puzzle.

The beach club's cheerful atmosphere matched the joy of their reunion. Conversations flowed, laughter filled the air, and the smell of the sea added to the scene. The golden afternoon sunlight spilled onto the sandy shore, creating the perfect setting to reconnect. Any awkwardness from their long-awaited meeting quickly faded as they shared smiles and warm embraces.

George, always charming, clapped Jim on the back and pulled him into a handshake that turned into a bear hug. "You've been away too long, Jim," he joked with a big smile. "I thought you forgot about us!"

Jim laughed and shook his head. "It's good to see you, George."

Meanwhile, Nancy hugged Ramona warmly, holding on longer than usual as if to make up for lost time. "You look amazing, Ramona," Nancy said with a palpable warmth. "It's been too long. Let's not let that happen again, okay?" Her words were filled with sincerity and love, adding to the warmth of the family reunion.

Ramona smiled, feeling warm inside from Nancy's kind words. "Agreed," she replied softly.

The conversation flowed easily, like waves on the shore. They talked about everything and nothing, sharing old memories and new updates. It felt natural as if the time since their last meeting didn't matter.

Lancy was shy at first and hid behind Ramona's leg. George bent down to her level, his eyes sparkling with fun. "Who is this little lady?" he asked playfully.

Lancy paused, then smiled slightly. "Lancy," she said, her voice soft but steady.

"Well, Miss Lancy," George said thoughtfully, "it's nice to meet you. How about we find some birds and feed them?"

George laughed as he took Lancy's tiny hand and led her to a group of seagulls at the beach. Jim followed closely with his camera, ready to take pictures. George and Jim showed Lancy how to toss crumbs to the birds. Lancy giggled as the seagulls flapped their wings and swooped down for the food, her joy growing with each toss.

Meanwhile, the women sat together in a shady spot on the patio. Rachael shared stories about her experience as a mother, mixing humor with some frustration. Nancy listened carefully and added funny comments about her social adventures. Their conversation flowed easily, filled with laughter and occasional looks toward the beach, where Lancy's laughter blended with the sounds of the seagulls.

As they talked, time flew by. They enjoyed the warmth of family, connecting old memories with new moments right before them. The sunset painted the beach club in golden light, and the air grew cooler as the day ended.

When it was time to say goodbye, George and Nancy were the first to leave. Their goodbyes were warm, just like their arrival. They hugged Ramona and Rachael tightly, and George quickly kissed Lancy on the forehead while she hugged his leg. "We need to do this more often," George said, sounding serious. Nancy smiled and nodded in agreement.

After George and Nancy left, the beach club became quieter. Only a few people stayed as evening came. Ramona and Rachael decided to take one last walk on the beach, with Lancy skipping ahead and laughing as the waves crashed nearby.

As they strolled side by side, Rachael broke the silence. "Mom would have cherished this, wouldn't she? She always loves our family outings, especially those by the beach."

Ramona nodded and looked at the horizon where the sun was setting. "She knew how to bring us together, didn't she? Even when things were hard, she made everything feel better."

Rachael smiled sadly but fondly. "I could almost hear her laughter today, especially when Dad was helping Lancy feed the birds. It felt like she was here with us, watching over us."

Ramona held Rachael's hand gently. "She lives on in every laugh and every cherished memory, Rachael. She is always with us."

They paused for a moment, both lost in thoughts of their mother. The cool evening breeze brought a sense of peace, as if their mother's spirit was near, offering them solace.

When Lancy called out to them from a distance, the sisters gave a knowing look. They silently acknowledged their mother's lasting influence on their lives. With warm hearts and fond memories, they turned to head back, carrying with them not just the memories of the day but also their mother's love, which continued to guide them.

They returned to Jim with smiles and contentment, ready to go home. They knew that the love their mother gave them would always keep them close.

# WHISPERS OF REFLECTION

The morning light filtered through the curtains, waking Ramona from her sleep. She felt tired, still weighed down by the laughter and late-night conversations from the day before. However, beneath her fatigue, there was a warm sense of happiness from being with her family. It was a gift she hadn't realized she needed.

She got out of bed quietly so she wouldn't wake anyone. Her feet moved toward the door, and her mind was restless. The peaceful world outside called to her, promising a quiet moment before the day began.

The garden welcomed her with a soft glow as the first rays of sunlight brightened everything around. The air was cool and carried a fresh scent of dew and earth. Ramona walked over to the old wooden bench by the rose bushes. As she sat down, the cool surface felt grounding. The garden, filled with wildflowers and neatly trimmed hedges, reminded her that life, while beautiful, is often messy.

Her fingers traced the worn leather cover of her journal, a familiar comfort in moments of solitude.

With a sense of reverence, she opened it, allowing her pen to hover over the blank page before she began to write.

"These moments—quiet and untouched by the rush of daily life—feel like stolen treasures. I still hear yesterday's laughter in my mind, but I also feel an ache, a sense of something unfinished."

She paused, remembering the day before.

This break was exactly what I needed; stepping away from the busy office has been refreshing. It's amazing how a change of scenery can help me see life differently. I've rediscovered the joy of being present and seeing the world with new wonder. I've also bonded more deeply with my family, something I didn't know I needed so much. This trip has been a gift, more meaningful than I expected.

*Observing Rachael and Jim's relationship stirred something profound within me. Their uncomplicated life and deep love for each other were a beacon of hope and inspiration, prompting me to ponder. Lancy's simple questions about life made me stop and think. How could I explain its complexities to her while still figuring them out myself? What I need now is a return to simplicity and a rejuvenated perspective.*

*My sister's words from yesterday echoed in my mind. Rachael's words brought Tom's memory rushing back, awakening emotions I thought were over. I had convinced myself that I had moved on from those emotions, like an old coat I no longer wear. Yet, as I sit here now, I realize that I miss not just him but the bond we shared. It could be the allure of this hometown, the nostalgia of being here, or witnessing Rachael's family life. Whatever the reason, it's rekindling emotions that I'm struggling to comprehend.*

*Ramona pen paused, and a thought came to her mind. For years, I've questioned if my practices—like morning walks, journaling, and meditation—were genuinely helping me grow. Am I changing, or just going through the motions to convince myself? Sitting here now, I feel I've found the answer. It's not just about the habits but who they've helped me become. I can appreciate the beauty in Rachael and Jim's love, connect with a stranger on the train, and strengthen my bond with Dad and Nancy—all of this comes from the foundation I've quietly built over time.*

*"Grateful for everything," she wrote."For the first time, I see the results of my silent labor—not in drastic changes, but in how I am beginning to open up, connect, and embrace life."*

*Ramona set down her pen and looked at the horizon. The rising sun painted the sky with shades of amber and rose, and the garden around her woke. A soft breeze rustled the leaves, bringing a sense of renewal.*

*She thought about the train ride here and her conversation with an older man who shared his thoughts on life. His words stuck with me: "Life is just a series of doors. Some you walk through, some close behind you, and some stand in front of, waiting until you're brave enough to knock."*

*"The picnic served as an opportunity for re connection," she wrote. I initially hesitated due to the emotional weight of reuniting with Dad and Nancy after a significant time apart. But now, it feels like a door I never realized I needed to open. Everything clicked, and the relief was undeniable— like a weight I didn't even know I was carrying had been lifted.*

*Ramona leaned back and rested the journal on her lap. The trip exceeded her hopes—it blended memories and new experiences of reconnecting and realizing things. The ache in her chest felt lighter now, not as sharp.*

The house was waking up—she heard the faint clink of dishes in the kitchen and voices. Ramona smiled softly and walked back inside. There was still much to think about, but for now, she was happy to let the day unfold.

The day passed peacefully, filled with unhurried moments and small tasks. Ramona kept herself busy finishing loose ends, including the legal paperwork to reconcile with her family officially. Each time she checked an item off her list, a sense of calm wrapped around her, as if her life was finding its place.

By late afternoon, Nancy called. Her cheerful voice instantly lifted Ramona's mood. Nancy shared how much everyone enjoyed the picnic and suggested, "We should do this more often."

Ramona held onto those words, feeling warmth in her chest. This new connection with her family felt like a gift she didn't know she needed. The idea of rebuilding these relationships and creating shared memories filled her with a deep sense of gratitude.

*Later that night, Ramona boarded the overnight train back to her city.*

The train's wheels clattered against the tracks, a steady sound that matched Ramona's thoughts. She sat by the window, her bag tucked under the seat and her journal on her lap. The cabin was dimly lit, and most passengers quietly talked or drifted off to sleep. Outside, the world blurred into fading twilight, sprinkled with lights from passing towns.

Ramona rested her head against the cool glass of the train window; her breath lightly misted the glass as she gazed at the horizon. The reunion felt like a dream, filled with warmth, laughter, and quiet moments. She loved those memories but couldn't shake the slight ache inside her—a mix of nostalgia and the awareness that life was moving on, pushing her forward whether she was ready.

Her journal lay open to a new page, and she held a pen, ready to write:

"The train feels like a place in between—neither here nor there, just a link between who I was this weekend and who I need to be when I return. Maybe that's what this trip was like—a link. It reminded me of the people who shaped me and the parts of myself I've forgotten. Seeing Rachael and Jim made me reflect—I've been so caught up in progress that I never paused to consider my destination.

She paused and looked out the window. The night seemed endless, with only the occasional glow of a streetlamp showing life beyond the tracks. The train's hum felt comforting as if the world held its breath with her.

Her thoughts turned to work, the endless deadlines and office politics waiting for her back in the city. The life she had built there felt distant now, much smaller than everything she had experienced in the last few days. Yet, under the worry, there was a hint of excitement—a curiosity about how she could apply what she had learned on this trip to her everyday life.

"Work will always be hectic," she wrote. "But maybe it doesn't have to take over my life. I can find moments of peace, like this one, even in the chaos."

As the train sped forward, Ramona closed her journal and leaned back in her seat, allowing herself to be present in the moment. She envisioned the city awaiting her, the people she would encounter, and the choices ahead of her. Her thoughts also drifted to Tom—his name flickered in her mind like a light she wasn't sure she wanted to illuminate.

# THE UNEXPECTED TURN

Ramona returned to the office feeling refreshed and ready to work. Her recent time away had energized her. Walking through the familiar halls, she noticed something was off. Instead of the usual chatter, there was an uncomfortable silence. Her co-workers, who usually welcomed her warmly, seemed to avoid eye contact. At first, she thought it was just Monday blues, but she sensed tension in the air.

When she reached her desk, she saw a notification on her screen: "Urgent Meeting" from HR. Ramona shut her laptop and went to the HR office, confused but not worried.

As Ramona settled into the plush chair in the small conference room, the HR manager approached her with a look of concern etched on his face. He offered a sincere apology, his voice slightly trembling as he spoke. Ramona's heart sank; the unease in the H R's eyes and the hesitance in tone immediately signaled that something unsettling was about to be revealed. The air was tense, and Ramona couldn't shake the feeling that she would receive news that would change everything.

"Ramona, I have some difficult news," the HR manager said softly. "Due to the company's recent restructuring, your position has been made redundant."

These words hit her hard, but Ramona stayed composed. While her mind raced, she nodded as she tried to understand this sudden change. The HR manager explained that this decision was not personal but a part of the company's new direction. You will receive severance pay for three months.

For a moment, time seemed to stop. Ramona had committed herself to her job and earned praise and recognition, but it was all gone. She struggled to believe what she heard. Just weeks ago, she had been celebrated for her contributions and praised by management for her ideas. Yet now, she was told she had no place in the company.

The HR manager's voice became a dull background sound. As Ramona considered the conversation, she registered only words like "pay" and "thanks." When she finally got up to leave, she felt numb, as if the weight of the discussion was pressing down on her.

She returned to her desk and looked at her things: framed photos, notebooks filled with ideas, and awards she had once been proud of. The space that used to feel familiar and energizing now seemed empty and strange. As the shock faded, a new feeling emerged—an unexpected sense of freedom. Maybe this was the universe pushing her to make the change she had been too scared to make alone.

As Ramona packed her things, her smile faded but remained. She felt sad about leaving behind a familiar place and was determined to seek new opportunities. Each item she placed in the box felt heavy with memories. A photo of her team at a holiday party reminded her of her friendships. A stack of notebooks, filled with her sketches and ideas, showed the many hours she had worked.

When a colleague approached her desk cautiously, Ramona prepared herself. "I just heard... I'm so sorry," they said quietly. Others glanced at her with sympathy but stayed away, unsure how to talk to her.

"It's okay," Ramona said with a smile. "I'll be fine."

At first, her words felt empty, but saying them out loud gave her a sense of control. As she carried her box out of the office, she held her head high and refused to let the situation bring her down.

* * *

When Ramona returned to her apartment, the reality of the day overwhelmed her. She placed the box in the corner of her living room and stared at it, unsure if she should unpack it or leave it as is. Ramona poured herself a glass of wine and sat on her couch while scrolling through her phone. Messages of support from friends and colleagues poured in, each expressing shock and encouragement.

*"Maybe this is a blessing in disguise," one friend texted. Another wrote, "You'll land on your feet. You always do."*

*She appreciated their words, but they felt distant and abstract. The biggest question in her mind was, What now?*

The city lights blinked outside her window, offering a comforting glow. Ramona realized she hadn't taken a moment to feel or process her loss. She closed her eyes and let the tears flow, each releasing the tension she had held all day.

The following days passed in a blur of disbelief and reflection. Ramona had seen layoffs before and watched as colleagues quietly packed their desks. However, she did not expect this to happen to her, especially after her recent achievements.

Elle, who used to be a close coworker, has kept her distance since the last office drama. Some coworkers reached out with kind words, but those calls quickly stopped. Bella, however, was always there for Ramona. She brought coffee and a positive attitude.

"That's life, Ramona," Bella said, trying to sound light while being understanding. "You'll get through this and probably come out stronger."

Ramona felt thankful for the support but wasn't quite ready to believe it. Her sister Rachael and brother-in-law Jim often called to cheer her up. They teased her about being a "rich woman now" and encouraged her to relax and enjoy her time off. Even her father, George, a well-known lawyer, suggested, "We can sue the company. They didn't give you proper notice—there's a case here."

Ramona responded firmly, "I don't want to get caught up in that negativity, Dad. It won't change anything."

Their kind words made her feel better, but Ramona knew she had to face this challenge alone. After years of a busy life—where even a single day off felt like a treat—she now woke up to find she had nowhere to go and nothing to do. The quiet felt strange, and the silence felt loud.

Ramona refused to let her job loss bring her down and immediately started job hunting. Confident in her experience, she updated her resume, refreshed her LinkedIn, and contacted former colleagues. But reality hit hard—employers favored younger candidates willing to work for less. As rejection emails piled up, her confidence began to fade.

Some interviews seemed promising but often ended with vague feedback about "going in another direction." Each rejection affected her confidence, questioning her professional value and ability to adapt to a changing industry.

Ramona felt frustrated and thought about working overseas, where her skills might be more valued. She spent hours looking for job opportunities abroad, writing cover letters for international positions, and learning about foreign business practices. However, the jobs she found didn't match her goals, and opportunities that once seemed promising now felt out of reach.

* * *

Weeks turned into months, and Ramona dealt with unemployment and a deep feeling of purposelessness. Mornings, which used to have a clear direction, now felt empty and slow. Despite this emptiness, she continued her daily routines—morning walks, journaling, and meditation. These simple habits helped her cope with her emotions.

Ramona recognized the significant impact her job had on her life.

Ramona recalls how, at times, she experienced frustration with her workplace, leading her to contemplate quitting in pursuit of new opportunities. However, these thoughts of leaving never materialized into actual decisions or actions. Now, she found herself without deadlines, the noise of a computer, or the coworkers she had seen more than her own family. They had all moved on, caught up in their lives as if she didn't exist anymore.

She knew it would be hard to adjust to these changes. But then again, she wasn't the only one fired. With this thought, she steeled herself to carry on and explore other aspects of life.

Unemployment gave Ramona a clear view of Tom's past struggles. She understood the quiet sadness he must have felt as his career declined. Back then, she was too focused on her goals to notice his frustrations, responding to his coldness with resentment. She realized how blind she had been. However, those moments were now in the past, beyond her reach.

Ramona refused to feel helpless. She joined sketching classes to reconnect with her creativity and worked on her programming skills to stay competitive. But as her savings shrank, she worried—how long could she stay in a city where costs kept rising?

Amongst all this chaos, a ray of silver lining appeared. She built connections in her classes, which led to small freelance projects. Though modest, these projects helped her meet her immediate needs.

Each task she completed was a step toward stability. She slowly created a routine from the quiet corners of her apartment, piecing together a fragile but hopeful sense of control amid the ongoing uncertainty.

# MEDITATION CAMP

As the days turned into months, Ramona gradually began to accept these new life terms, and a sense of contentment settled within her.

One morning, she received an unexpected email from the meditation camp. It said her application had been accepted, and she could attend the next session. "Your response is awaited," it said.

Surprised by the message, she realized she had forgotten about enrolling in the camp a few months back.

Is this necessary right now, when everything is finally falling into place? She wondered. Bella strongly recommended the experience—a week of silence, meditation, and simple living without phones or distractions. It would undoubtedly be trans formative. If not now, then when? she finally reasoned.

After rechecking her work schedule, Ramona confirms her attendance for the upcoming session.

Ramona had taken a leap of faith and signed up for the camp, embracing the freedom that came with being a freelancer. The idea of making spontaneous decisions and exploring new possibilities felt liberating—something that her regular job life would never have allowed. Taking a week off on a whim was a distant dream, but now, it was a reality.

The camp was located on the city's outskirts, nestled among farmlands. As the taxi veered off the highway and onto the narrow country lanes, Ramona began to feel a growing sense of unease. The once-open road led to winding paths lined with tall, overgrown bushes. There were hardly any other cars in sight, and the lane seemed to shrink with each turn.

Her confidence began to fade, and self-doubt crept in. Am I heading in the right direction? Is this place safe? she thought, nervously looking at her phone. The signal had dropped just when she needed it most. A thought crossed her mind—Should I turn back?With her fingers crossed, Ramona hoped the camp was nearby. Finally, after an eternity, the taxi slowed as it neared camp.

Ramona's heart raced as she took in the camp's serene beauty. Nestled at the end of a winding road surrounded by tall trees and farmland, the camp was breathtaking, but the scene did little to calm her nerves. A worn wooden sign welcomed her: "Meditation Retreat—Welcome."

As the taxi stopped, Ramona paused before getting out. Her legs felt shaky on the gravel path. It was very quiet, different from the busy city she knew. The only sounds were leaves rustling and birds chirping, but she felt nervous. She wondered if this was a mistake. What if she didn't belong here?

She rechecked her phone—there was no signal. "Great," she laughed nervously. There was no turning back now.

Ramona stood there, unsure. She had imagined a busy camp with people like her looking for peace, but it was empty.

Am I the only one here? she thought, looking around at the vast open space. Some of her wanted to ask the taxi driver to wait if she changed her mind, but he had already driven off, kicking up dust as if deciding her fate.

She sighed deeply. There was no turning back now—no way out. She could either make the most of this experience or spend the next few days regretting her choice. I wanted freedom, didn't I? she reminded herself. This is it-uncharted, raw, and authentic.

She lifted her shoulders and took a deep breath, trying to calm her nerves. However, as she walked toward the camp, her mind remained confused.

What if I don't belong here? What if this journey brings up feelings I'm not ready to deal with?

Yet, amidst these uncertainties, a quieter, more steadfast thought began to surface: What if this was precisely what I needed? The chance for growth and self-discovery called out to her.

With renewed determination, she moved forward, ready to embrace whatever this experience had in store.

Upon entering the office, she was given a form to complete and asked to place her phone, valuables, and any other distracting items in a designated area. A sigh of relief escaped her as she noticed other participants around her. Afterward, she was guided to her room—a simple space with a bed and a small bathroom. Other participants were still checking in, and she found herself intrigued by the sight of some younger faces, wondering what had led them to seek peace at such a tender age.

She explored the property and observed the vast farmland, beautifully maintained with lush greenery. The Camp had different sections: a common meditation hall, a dining area, and others. The men had their separate sections.

In the evening, a helper with a bell signaled for the participants to gather in the assembly hall. About fifty participants of different ages came together. The teachers introduced themselves and explained the camp's rules again. Then, everyone took a vow of silence and went to the meditation hall, where their assigned seats were ready for the session.

The meditation hall was an ample, circular space with a high ceiling, creating an atmosphere of serenity. The stillness was palpable. Participants were instructed to sit cross-legged, close their eyes, and focus on their breath.

Ramona was used to meditating, but doing it in this dome with a group of strangers felt different and uncomfortable. Meditation had always been her refuge, done alone in her familiar room. Being around others in this vast dome made her feel more unsettled than expected.

The room's circular shape seemed to amplify every sound, from the soft rustling of fabric to the quiet sighs of breathing. Even her movements felt magnified, making her hesitant to change her posture, afraid she would shatter the silence.

Despite her efforts to focus, Ramona's thoughts drifted. Why can't I relax? Why does this feel so different?

The unfamiliar atmosphere was calm yet energetic, leaving her feeling off balance. Back home, meditation was something she controlled and used as a safe space to escape the chaos of her life. However, it felt more profound and demanding here, as if the room required her full attention and surrender.

The group dynamic made things more complicated. While they were supposed to create shared energy, Ramona felt like an outsider. Everyone else looked calm and steady while she dealt with the pain in her back, the tingling in her legs, and the doubts in her mind. "Am I the only one finding this hard?" she thought, looking at the other participants.

As the session continued, she focused on breathing and tried to stay present, but her mind wouldn't settle. Instead, worry took over: How would she endure a full day of this tomorrow? The thought hit her—this was just the start.

When the bell rang, Ramona opened her eyes, relieved and nervous. Around her, others got up from their meditation, moving slowly and looking calm. She, however, felt anything but peaceful. Her body felt stiff, her mind was restless, and she had a tight knot of doubt in her chest.

As the group quietly left the hall, Ramona stayed behind momentarily, looking at the unlit candle in the middle of the room. Can I do this? she wondered. The thought of meditating an entire day—sitting still, facing herself, and dealing with this intensity—seemed overwhelming.

But as she got up and followed the others to the dining area, a quieter thought came to her mind, and she held onto it despite her doubts: Maybe it's supposed to be this hard. Maybe that's the point.

The camp followed a strict schedule, with dinner at sunset and morning tea at sunrise, starkly contrasting with city life's bustling rhythm. An hour before tea, the morning bell marked the beginning of their day in silence, a practice so foreign to Ramona's urban routine.

The group silently gathered in the dining area, each person settling into their designated spot with utensils. The meal was simple yet nourishing, providing just enough to satisfy. They were instructed to give their full attention to every task—whether eating or washing their dishes—and remain fully present in the moment.

After dinner, they went back to their rooms. Night had fallen, and it was very dark. As Ramona lay on her bed, the quiet felt deep, broken only by the soft humming of mosquitoes outside her window.

The silence of the night made Ramona uneasy. It was so different from the usual noise of city life. She glanced at the window, where she saw a lizard moving across the glass. Even though there was a protective net, watching its slow movements made her uncomfortable. The dim light outside and the quiet buzzing of mosquitoes added to her growing worry.

The activities of the day made her very tired. Even though it was quiet and the lizard was nearby, she couldn't fight her fatigue. Soon, she fell fast asleep.

# TRUTH IN SILENCE

Ramona woke up to the soft sound of a distant bell. Its chime was gentle and comforting. For a moment, she wasn't sure if night had already ended. It felt as though she had only just fallen asleep, her dreams still fresh in her mind. She lay still, wrapped in the quiet, not yet ready to release the warmth of sleep.

Looking through the small, frosted window, she saw darkness outside. The night sky was still, with only a few lights flickering like tiny fireflies. People passed her quiet spot, their footsteps soft on the cool floor, as if they didn't want to break the morning calm. The distant bell rang again, calling them to the first session of the day.

Shivering in the cold morning air, Ramona dressed quickly and stepped outside. The quiet was so deep that every movement felt loud. Her footsteps crunched on the gravel, the sound sharp in the stillness. She hugged herself against the chill, a wave of unease creeping in. But the steady ringing of the bell gave her something to focus on, leading her toward the hall.

Inside, the hall was filling up. Participants crept, their faces serious as they found their seats. Helpers watched closely to keep everyone silent, reminding them of the discipline required. Ramona took her place, crossing her legs as the room filled with a noticeable stillness.

When she closed her eyes, the atmosphere changed completely. Meditation was a personal escape at home—easygoing, with distractions and no pressure to be perfect. But in the dimly lit dome, with focused people around her, the group's energy sparked an intensity she didn't expect. The stillness of the early morning made the experience feel even more potent as if the world paused to highlight this critical moment.

She focused on her breath, noticing each inhale and exhale blending with the deep silence around her. Time seemed to lose its relevance. She no longer saw her body, forgetting the tension in her shoulders and the ache in her back. The calmness of her breath felt soothing, like waves on a shore.

When the clear and strong bell rang again, it marked the end of the session. She slowly opened her eyes as if waking from a vivid dream, and the world came back into view. Snapping back to reality felt confusing, leaving her unsure if it had been a peaceful escape or a flood of emotions.

The group quietly walked to the dining area for breakfast. Outside, the world had come alive, glowing in the soft light of early morning. Ramona stopped for a moment, captivated by the peaceful beauty around her. Dewdrops sparkled on the grass, and a gentle breeze carried a faint, sweet scent of flowers. Birds sang together in the distance, their songs blending as if welcoming the new day. A peacock walked through the farmland, its colorful feathers spreading slowly and proudly. The scene was almost too perfect, highlighting the unease that stirred within her.

At breakfast, Ramona sat with the others. They all shared a quiet moment. She looked at their faces; some were familiar from the meditation hall, while others were new. Each person seemed calm and mindful as they ate. However, Ramona suspected some of them also struggled with doubts, just like she did. She couldn't be the only one feeling this way. Could she?

She considered the long day ahead. The plan was clear: many hours of meditation, interrupted only by short breaks for rest or meals. However, it felt overwhelming and hard to handle. She fidgeted with her spoon, struggling to enjoy the calm around her.

The teacher's words from orientation returned to her: The first two days will be difficult. Your mind will fight against it, your body will hurt, and doubts will arise. But if you are patient, you will find peace. Keep going, and you will discover a rhythm.

The second meditation session began, and Ramona found it challenging to settle. The dome's high ceiling magnified every slight sound—the rustling of cushions, a muffled cough, the quiet creak of a floorboard. She shifted in her seat, feeling the numbness creep into her legs and the stiffness tighten her back. Helpers moved silently through the room, offering extra cushions and back support to those who needed them. Some received chairs for added comfort, but despite these adjustments, the discomfort lingered, making it hard to focus.

Ramona closed her eyes and tried to focus, but her thoughts danced around chaotically, slipping away like sand through her fingers. Her breath became shallow, and her concentration faded. The pain in her legs grew more substantial, and she fought the urge to move, afraid to break the silence.

How will I get through this? she wondered. The memory of the peaceful morning landscape felt far away as if it belonged to another world. The promise of calm and clarity seemed out of reach, hidden under discomfort and frustration.

As the session continued, Ramona realized she wasn't just dealing with physical pain—she was facing herself in a new way. Without distractions, her mind had nowhere to go, and this confrontation felt as uncomfortable as the meditation position she struggled to hold.

The teacher's words echoed again: This is the storm before the calm. Push through. For now, those words were her anchor, the small hope she clung to in a sea of doubt.

It was hard to keep going—her mind wandered, her body hurt, and each second felt like a test. The sound of the bell for a break was the only relief, a chance to sit up straight, stretch her muscles, and breathe easily for a moment. Still, it helped to know she wasn't alone in this struggle—everyone around her faced their challenges silently. They were all united by a shared search for something more profound.

After a long day of discomfort and frustration, the evening discourse session provided relief. When the projector turned on, it lit the room with a warm, welcoming glow. An older lady appeared on the screen, her calm and understanding face showing a lifetime of experience. Her steady and warm voice felt like a comforting hug, creating a safe space for everyone to set aside their exhaustion and worries. She clearly understood the day's struggles, and her soothing presence encouraged everyone to listen.

The older woman spoke gently, her voice a soothing break from the day's stress. "This program gives you a glimpse into a monk's life," she said. "At its heart, it's about discovering the truth. To help you understand, let me share an old fable."

Once, four men who had been blind since birth were asked to touch an elephant and describe their feelings. Each man touched a different part: the trunk, the tail, the tusk, and the side. Their descriptions were very different. One thought the elephant was like a rope, and another thought it was like a tree trunk, and so on. Each man was sure of his view, but none saw the complete truth."

Our experiences, including family and society, shape our understanding of truth. Over time, the clarity of truth becomes blurred by the lies we tell others and, more dangerously, the lies we tell ourselves. These distortions affect how we see the world, leading to twisted perceptions.

In this quiet space, we practice silence away from everyday distractions. Silence is not just the absence of sound but a state of mind that allows us to listen to our inner voice. Being calm helps us avoid spreading or listening to false information and meaningless talk. By looking inward, we start to clear our minds, removing confusion and clutter that can hide our true insight. This self-exploration allows us to face our thoughts and feelings honestly, which helps us understand ourselves better. We can see reality more clearly as we break down these mental barriers. This clarity lets us accept truth in its most genuine form, guiding our actions and shaping our views.

Ramona felt a tightness in her chest as the woman's words sank in. Lies. That word echoed in her mind, breaking through the confusion. Hadn't she been holding on to twisted truths about her job, her relationship with Tom, and even about herself? These 'twisted truths' were not outright lies but somewhat distorted versions of reality that she had convinced herself were accurate. They had been her mask and her protection, a way to cope. But now, in this silent space, she had nowhere to hide. The retreat was stripping away the layers she had built over the years, forcing her to face the harsh truth underneath.

The realization hit her harder than she anticipated. For the first time, everything clicked—the unhappiness with her job, the hurt from her breakup, the constant search for meaning. In this quiet moment, clarity started to appear. The understanding she had been seeking for so long was finally here as if waiting for her to absorb. She understood how tangled she had become with the lies that had kept her in the dark and how the old wisdom of silence, mindfulness, and reflection was the key to unraveling it all.

"Ramona deeply appreciated the camp's simplicity and authenticity. The quietness reached a part of her she had long neglected, offering a gentle reminder of what she had been missing. This experience wasn't just a getaway but a chance to rediscover herself."

Ramona felt a deep sense of gratitude as she thought about Bella. A simple thank you wouldn't be enough—Bella had recognized Ramona's struggles before seeing them herself.

Ramona decided to call Bella when she got back. There was so much she wanted to share, but mostly, she wanted to thank her for guiding her on this journey—for helping her find her way back to herself.

# FINDING BALANCE

Ramona felt the weight of self-doubt and uncertainty lift as if heavy clouds had parted to reveal a sky of clarity and acceptance. It was like stepping out of a dense fog that had surrounded her for so long. The world around her seemed transformed—colors appeared more prosperous, sounds sharper, and every sensation more vivid and alive. Happiness and contentment filled each moment, lingering beside her like faithful companions."

Even the lizard resting by her window, which she once found unsettling, now represented peaceful coexistence. It reminded her of her strength to accept life as it is, with all its imperfections and challenges. Feeling this new peace that night, she fell into a deep and restful sleep.

The following day, she observed that her neighbor's room was locked, prompting her to consider whether they had moved on. As the day progressed, Ramona felt more focused during her meditation practice. Her persistent body aches became more manageable, and she embraced them as a natural part of her journey toward growth and healing.

A full day of meditation and a vow of silence opened her eyes to a new world. Stripped of her phone, TV, and conversations, she witnessed the relentless pace at which people chased their desires, often missing the beauty of the present moment.

"Lost in her mind, she watched helplessly as her thoughts rose and fell like ocean waves. At first, each one surfaced gently, seeming harmless—but the more she focused on them, the heavier they became. They gathered emotions, old memories, and feelings she had buried for too long. It was unsettling to witness their transformation, to feel the exact moment when simple ideas turned into powerful forces shaping her choices and actions."

"As the day progressed, Ramona faced the silence around her—and within her. At first, her mind resisted, swirling with memories, tasks, and worries. She realized she had been avoiding stillness, constantly staying busy as if quietness were something to fear. This awareness marked a significant step in her journey of self-discovery and mindfulness."

"Ramona reflected on her breakup with Tom. She had often held onto frustration and resentment, allowing them to grow into arguments instead of letting them go. Now, as she revisited the memory, regret surfaced—but rather than being consumed by it, she simply observed, offering herself the grace to understand and move forward."

As she sat in silence, Ramona remembered her mother. When she was seven, she walked to school holding her mother's hand. It was a simple morning, but Ramona remembered asking, "Why are we walking so slow?"

Her mother smiled and said, "If we rush, we'll miss all the beautiful things around us."

Years later, in the stillness of the retreat, Ramona finally understood. She had spent so much time chasing goals and filling every moment with activity that she had overlooked the beauty around her. Only now did her mother's words genuinely resonate.

Tears welled up in her eyes. She had spent so long in a rush, and now, in this silence, she finally grasped the essence. It wasn't just about slowing down but about seeing, feeling, and truly living in the moment. Her mother had always tried to instill this kind of presence in her.

Ramona opened her eyes. She felt her mother's wisdom sink deep into her heart.

It was time for our discourse. The projector was set, and an elderly lady with a subtle, calming voice appeared on the screen. She began, "By now, most of us may have felt a bit of silence, a sense of peace enter our lives. For those who haven't yet, just believe in the process."

She paused momentarily to let her words sink in before continuing, "Our minds work in a certain way. As we go through our daily lives, we face many choices. Some choices are small, like deciding what to eat, while others are big, like choosing a career. In every situation, two main things shape our choices: the intelligence we gain from our experiences and our deep emotions."

The woman smiled gently and looked thoughtful. "Think of making decisions like driving a car. Intelligence and emotions are like the driver and co-driver. We often think that intelligence—our logic and experience—drives the car, while emotions sit beside the driver's seat, giving subtle directions."

She leaned in slightly as if sharing a secret. "But if you think about your life, you might see that emotions often take control of the wheel. Instead of being in charge, intelligence and experience end up in the passenger seat, adjusting to the emotional driver's impulses."

"Her voice softened, and she looked directly at the audience through the screen. "Take a moment to reflect on this. Think about a recent decision you made, whether at work or in your personal life. Now ask yourself, did your intelligence guide that decision? Or were your emotions leading you in ways that logic couldn't explain?"

A quiet buzz filled the room as her words made the participants think. "Maybe you've done more work because you want to show something to others or yourself. Or maybe you held back from taking a risk because you were scared or unsure, even though part of you knew it was the right choice. These examples show how emotions can quietly take control."

Her tone became more positive. "The great thing about this retreat is that we're learning to notice when our emotions take control. Once we notice that, we can guide them back to their proper place as helpers. It's not about pushing away emotions—they are important—but about finding a balance with reason. This way, we can make clear decisions instead of acting impulsively."

With practice, you will find harmony. The driver and co-driver can work together as a team, each doing their part. This is not a fixed state but a journey of growth and improvement each of you can embark on.

As the elderly lady's words filled the room, Ramona sat quietly, her back straight and hands resting in her lap. The calm atmosphere of the meditation retreat eased some of the tension she had felt before, but the lady's words struck a deeper chord.

As the lady spoke about balancing intelligence and emotions, Ramona thought about her life. Her mind drifted to her breakup with Tom. She had convinced herself it was the right decision—they had indeed begun to grow apart. Now, listening to the metaphor of the driver and co-driver, she wondered: Had her emotions been in charge of the breakup? Had her frustration, impatience, and unspoken fears taken control while her intelligence just sat beside her, like a co-driver in a car, unable to act but still there, ready to take over when needed?

Her thoughts drifted back to the months after her mother's death. She had partied, stayed out late, and made impulsive choices at work. At the time, these seemed like ways to cope, but now she saw that her emotions were driving her actions, worsening her inner struggle.

Ramona shifted in her seat, realizing how valid the elderly lady's words were. The emotions she tried to hide often influenced her most significant decisions, and her rational mind, which she had always trusted to guide her decisions based on logic and reason, just went along with it.

As the truth dawned on her, Ramona felt relief wash over her. For the first time, she realized this retreat was not about ignoring or pushing her feelings aside. It was about recognizing when her emotions took over and learning to regain control.

She understood that both her thoughts and feelings are essential in making decisions. This discovery gave her a new sense of balance and ignited a spark of hope for finding peace between the two. She felt inspired and motivated to continue her journey of self-discovery.

She promised herself to think more deeply about this. Looking around the room, she noticed others lost in their thoughts, and for the first time in a while, she felt she wasn't alone in this challenge. It comforted her that everyone here was also trying to understand their emotions and find a way to balance them. This shared struggle brought a sense of connection and understanding that she had been missing.

# FROM KNOWLEDGE TO UNDERSTANDING

With each passing day, Ramona began to feel more comfortable in camp life. The simplicity, silence, and strict routine that once felt overwhelming now gave her a sense of freedom. Her small, plain room became a place of peace instead of a prison, and the vow of silence no longer felt like a limit but a way to escape the noise of everyday life.

In the early morning, Ramona noticed details she used to miss—the gentle sounds of the world waking up, the soft rustling of leaves, and the songs of birds. As she sat quietly, she wondered about the bird's communication. In those moments, she felt a change, as if she were seeing the world with new eyes, free from the constant clutter of thoughts.

Before coming to camp, Ramona thought of it as a prison. She saw silence and stillness as burdens to bear instead of gifts to enjoy. Bella, however, loved this setting and appreciated the peace around them. Ramona wanted to test herself and saw this experience as a survival challenge. But once she settled in, she realized how wrong that idea was.

This experience was not about being firm but a chance to let go of bad habits and move past one old self. Ramona understood that the freedom she felt was more profound than words. She was free from the noise, stress, and constant thoughts that used to overwhelm her. She found clarity and strength in this peaceful place, embracing the change from letting go and being present.

During the day's meditation, this newfound understanding began to crystallize. As the group sat silently, the old lady—a figure of kindness and firmness—began to speak. Her gentle voice, filled with significance, resonated throughout the room.

"Your meditation is getting deeper," she said, looking around the room before settling on Ramona. "In our last session, we discussed balancing feelings and logic. Today, we will go further. Think about how our consciousness works—it is not random, but strongly tied to our survival."

"We come into this world fragile and completely reliant on others. The old lady continued, her voice calm but purposeful. As we grow older, we become stronger and more resilient. In our prime, we are driven by strong desires and the instinct to nurture and create new life. But as time passes, our strength fades, and we become vulnerable again near the end of our lives. This is the cycle of life—a continuous rhythm that does not stop."

Ramona had heard this before from textbooks and conversations. But now, at the camp, it felt different. It was no longer just about biology; it connected to the more profound wisdom of life. In the quiet surroundings, free from distractions, she understood this truth in a new way. It was not just an idea but something alive and real inside her.

The room was heavy with silence, yet the old lady's words lingered in the air, carrying the weight of deep emotion. Ramona's thoughts drifted to the poignant chapters of her life—the stinging sorrow of losing her mother, the deep ache of her breakup with Tom, and the unsettling feeling of everything falling apart.

As the old lady spoke, Ramona began to see her wounds not as lonely struggles but as small parts of the larger story of life. This understanding felt vast and shared, going beyond her own experience. With this new perspective, she felt an unexpected warmth that eased the sharpness of her grief. She realized that her experiences, though personal, were part of a universal human journey, which brought a sense of belonging and understanding.

"We humans," the old lady said, "create communities, build things, and give meaning to our lives. Some people seek knowledge, while others want wealth. Our goals differ, but the way we pursue them is similar."

She paused, her eyes appearing to see beyond the moment. "Imagine a man walking through a dark jungle. He is lost and scared of the unknown—afraid of the wilderness, the animals around him, and the loneliness. As night goes on, he worries he might not survive until morning. Then, in the dim moonlight, he sees another man sitting under a tree. At first, he wonders if he's imagining it—but it's real.

The old lady leaned closer, her gaze firm. "Feeling relieved, he walks up to the man and says, 'I'm so glad to find you. I was lost and scared, unsure how to make it through the night.' The other man, also feeling relieved, replies, 'I understand. I'm lost too.'"

"They were still lost in the jungle, and their situation hadn't changed, but something felt different. Together, they found hope by being there for each other, forming a connection during a scary time.

Her voice softened as she said, "Isn't that how life is? We don't know where it starts or how it will end. Life is like a race. We receive a baton from the previous generation. We run our part, complete our time, and then pass it on to the next. We may not always have the answers during this journey, but we find comfort and meaning in being together. With all its uncertainty, the journey feels easier when we share it."

Ramona listened quietly to the old lady's words. She began to understand the deep wisdom that had been hard to grasp. Her journey to this camp—the doubts, the unease—now felt like layers she was shedding. She had come to the retreat seeking a challenge that would test her limits, but instead, she found something much more humbling. It wasn't just about staying silent or proving her strength; it was about accepting simplicity and allowing herself to be still so that deeper truths could emerge.

The story about the two men lost in the jungle struck a chord in her. It reminded her of times when she felt lost in her own life. She struggled with the boredom of her job, dealt with the sadness of her breakup with Tom, and faced the deep grief of losing her mother. She had been navigating her jungle, often so focused on surviving that she missed the quiet hope around her. However, sitting in the stillness of the camp, she could see things more clearly.

The old lady's words about life being a cycle, passed down through generations, moved her significantly. She had always simply understood this idea—she read about it and heard it from others—but now it felt real and personal. She realized her mother's death was not just a singular event; it was part of a more significant cycle. Her mother had passed on the baton to her, and someday, she would pass it on, too—through her work, relationships, or how she carried herself in life. Everything was connected.

Ramona felt a strange sense of peace. The pain of loss and life's challenges were still there, but they felt lighter and more manageable. Like the two men in the jungle, she was navigating the unknown, but she wasn't alone. She had Bella, Rachael, and the people at the camp, all on their journeys but walking beside her.

In that moment, Ramona realized something important. She moved from just thinking about life to truly understanding it. The jungle, the wilderness, and the nights represent the struggles and uncertainties everyone faces. Just as the two men found comfort in each other, she began to find comfort in connection and in the shared experience of being human.

As the meditation session ended, Ramona took a deep breath and felt grateful. She had come to the camp looking for something outside herself, but she had found a more profound connection within. It was no longer about just surviving the wilderness; it was about learning to walk through it with grace, an open heart, and the understanding that no one truly walks alone.

# REDISCOVERING LOVE AND BELONGING

The meditation camp has ended. The vow of silence has been lifted, and participants begin to retrieve their phones and other belongings from the small wooden storage area. Although the signal in the remote location is still weak, holding her cell phone feels strange to Ramona—like picking up something from a life she has left behind.

After days of silence, talking again was a unique experience. However, when Ramona first spoke, her voice surprised her. It was familiar but felt different as if she was just starting to discover herself. Each word felt important and new, reminding her of the deep stillness she had experienced over the past few days.

As conversations spread through the camp, she felt drawn to the voices of others. What was once just noise now carried meaning. The faces she had quietly watched during meditation became lively with stories and personality.

The group surprised Ramona with its beautiful tapestry of diversity. It included an aspiring teacher, a retired army officer, a politician, a farmer, a hotel owner, and various professionals. They all came together, bringing unique experiences and perspectives and forming a vibrant community.

Over cups of tea from the communal kitchen, they shared their thoughts on the camp and offered different views on life. Their stories, each a unique thread in the fabric of their shared experience, added depth and understanding to the journey. Some found the camp meaningful, while others saw it as a temporary experience, something to think about but not life-changing.

One story stuck with Ramona. A woman in her 50s talked about her long struggle with insomnia. "I've tried every pill and every therapy," she said, her voice showing both hope and sadness. "The stillness here helped. I know I can close my eyes without fear, even briefly." Her words resonated because she found peace in her struggle, even if she hadn't completely overcome her sleeplessness.

People talked about how hard it was to maintain their newfound calm. Some worried that the peace would slip away once they returned to their busy lives—filled with work, family, and responsibilities. Small groups formed, exchanging phone numbers and taking photos, including a few cheerful group selfies. But beneath the laughter, a quiet worry remained. The stillness they had created felt delicate like morning mist disappearing with the first rays of sunlight.

A voice rose above the chatter and the soft clinking of glasses.

"It feels like being at a funeral," someone said. "In that sacred space, you're bound together by shared grief, by something deeper than words. But the moment you step outside, into the bright, indifferent world, those feelings dissolve—leaving only a faint echo behind."

Ramona nodded in agreement. She felt the same way. She had lived at a different pace for days, focused on silence and simplicity. But now, the outside world called to her, bringing noise, demands, and distractions.

A woman who returned to the retreat for the third time in five years shared her thoughts. She recognized that many people worry the benefits of learning might fade when they return to their busy lives. However, she pointed out that those who genuinely practice meditation as a way of living can keep the lessons with them.

"You can always redo the session," she said with a friendly smile. "Every time, it feels like discovering something new. The experience becomes richer, even though the lessons are the same."

Her words showed her personal experience, but she clarified that the outcome depends on individual effort. "It's not easy," she said thoughtfully. "Five participants left mid-session. They couldn't continue, and that's okay. Meditation isn't about pushing yourself but finding your own pace.

As the retreat ended, participants started saying goodbye. Taxis arranged to take everyone to different places, and they exchanged warm farewells. Some people hugged for a long time, while others promised to keep in touch.

They all felt hopeful but a bit cautious. Everyone knew the peace they found during the retreat would be tested once they returned to their busy lives. Still, as they parted, they felt determined to hold on to some calm they had experienced.

* * *

As Ramona entered her apartment, she noticed the stark contrast between the calm she had experienced at the retreat and the bustling city life. The silence that had comforted her now felt heavy, a stark contrast to the peaceful serenity of the retreat. It was interrupted by the loud buzzing of her fridge and the distant traffic sounds. Her phone kept pinging, breaking the quiet she was trying to maintain.

She stopped in the doorway, her retreat bag still on her shoulder. A stack of unopened mail and packages sat on the counter, seeming to accuse her of neglect. The blinking notifications on her phone called for her attention.

For a moment, she felt stuck. The peace she had found during her retreat seemed fragile, hanging by a thread. The air in her apartment felt thicker and almost suffocating. She realized she was holding her breath, struggling to maintain the tranquility she had found. Instead of dealing with everything at once, she decided to head to her small balcony for some fresh air.

Ramona settled into her favorite chair, wrapped in a soft throw. The night sky surrounded her. A bright star stood out against the darkness, reminding her of the calm she felt after the retreat. She took a deep breath of the cool evening air. Even though she could hear the city in the distance, she felt free from its demands.

For a moment, she thought about Bella, who was still traveling. She wanted to share her retreat experience and hear Bella's excited responses. The idea made Ramona smile and looked forward to their following chat. For now, she enjoyed this quiet moment alone.

Her eyes glanced at her phone on the side table. It glowed softly and seemed to call to her. She picked it up, her fingers hesitating as if it were something from long ago. "Oh, dear friend, I did miss you," she said with a smile.

The screen lit up with missed calls and unread messages. One message stood out: a photo from Rachael. Curious, Ramona opened it. The picture showed her sister, husband, daughter, father, and Nancy at the family home. The caption read: "Really miss you, sis. I'm at Dad's house. I tried to contact you, but I know about the strict camp policies."

As she looked at the photo, Ramona felt a tightness in her chest. A tear fell down her cheek. This time, it was not from confusion or sadness but from gratitude. She was thankful for the love that connected her to these people, no matter how far away she was.

She remembered the last time Rachael sent her a photo like this one. The memory struck her hard, causing a deep ache inside. At that time, the image reminded her of the distance from her family and made her feel more alone. Each smiling face seemed to tease her, showing a happy life she no longer shared. But now, something changed as she looked at their faces in the picture.

The smiles still held warmth, but now they made her feel like she belonged. She didn't feel like an outsider anymore. She felt connected to their love, as if she was part of their lives, even from a distance. The retreat had helped her lower the walls she built around herself, allowing this connection to grow.

Ramona wiped her cheek with a steady hand. She had come a long way—from wanting connection to accepting it. She typed a reply to Rachael with a calmness she hadn't felt in years. Her fingers moved quickly: "Thank you for this. I miss you all, too. Let's talk soon—I can't wait to catch up."

She hit send and leaned back in the chair, looking up at the star again. She closed her eyes and let gratitude wash over her. She had completed the retreat, but more importantly, she had returned to herself.

Ramona smiled through her tears and strongly wanted to share her feelings with someone. *Bella came to her mind. Before she could call, her phone buzzed. It was Bella. Ramona couldn't help laughing at the timing.*

*Ramona: "Bella! It's so good to hear your voice right now."*

*Bella: "I've been waiting for your call. So, how was it? Did the silence help you or not?"*

*Ramona: "It was both, I think. The first few days were hard—I felt restless. But then something changed. The silence helped me think more clearly without all the noise of life."*

*Bella: "I knew it! That's what I hoped for you. Do you feel different now?"*

*Ramona: "Yes, I do. It feels like I've had this tight knot for ages, and it's finally starting to loosen. I kept thinking about you while I was there. You always find balance. I think I finally understand that now."*

*Bella: "That's nice to hear, but don't give me too much credit. I have my moments, too. I'm happy you're feeling this way. What surprised you most about the retreat?"*

*Ramona: "Honestly? I learned a lot just by watching people. When you don't talk, you notice things—like body language, how someone pours tea, or how they sit when lost in thought. It's a whole world I ignored before. The stories people shared afterward were raw and beautiful. It made me realize I've been isolating myself. I don't want to do that anymore."*

*Bella: "That's great, Ramona. You've been through a lot. I'm proud of you for wanting to connect again. I'm always here for you, right?"*

*Ramona: "I know. I'm thankful for you, Bella. Who else would have pushed me to do something out of my comfort zone? You believed in me when I didn't believe in myself."*

*Bella: "That's what friends do. I always knew you had this in you—you just needed a little push. So, what's next? How will you keep this newfound wisdom alive?"*

*Ramona: "Good question. I'm not sure yet. I think I want to keep meditating.*

*Bella: "That sounds good. Just take it one step at a time, okay? No need to fix everything right away."*

*Ramona: "I will. Thank you, Bella. For everything."*

*Bella: "Always. Now go get some rest—you sound happy, but you need rest after all that self-discovery."*

*Ramona: "You're right. I'll call you soon, okay? I can't wait to catch up."*

*Bella: "I'm looking forward to it. Love you."*

*Ramona: "Love you too."*

*As the call ended, Ramona put her phone down with a smile. Bella's belief in her had been the nudge she didn't know she needed. Leaning back in her chair, she let the city's noise fade away, focusing on her breathing.*

# ECHOES OF THE PAST

A week passed as Ramona worked to catch up on the many tasks that piled up while she was away at the meditation camp. The experience stayed with her, changing her in subtle ways. She felt more fit now, with a new sense of energy. Her face showed a calmness that caught the attention of her colleagues and even strangers. However, beneath this calm surface, her inner world had changed profoundly.

Ramona became more thoughtful and quieter than she used to be. The hours spent in meditation revealed uncomfortable truths. Most shocking was how common deception is in daily life. She noticed how easily she told little lies to make social interactions smoother or avoid awkward moments. It wasn't just her noticing this. She saw it all around: the half-truths in meetings, the fake politeness of neighbors, and the empty promises in advertisements. It felt like society had tolerated and embraced this web of lies to keep things running smoothly. This realization made her profoundly uncomfortable and disillusioned.

Despite her inner transformation, Ramona was acutely aware that she could not completely detach from the demands of modern life, even as a freelancer. Although she could set her schedule and choose projects that fueled her creativity, she faced pressure from deadlines, client demands, and competition in her field. Although single and had no family obligations, she felt connected to the world's expectations, a stark contrast to the inner peace she was striving for.

The retreat had awakened in Ramona a longing for something more in her life. She didn't want to abandon her life but to make it more authentic. She longed to carry the clarity and honesty of her meditation into her daily routine—a challenge in a world that seldom embraced such openness. Yet, the awareness she gained acted like a guide, gently leading her to respond kindly to emails, consider before taking on projects that didn't match her values, and appreciate small moments like enjoying a cup of tea.

Ramona couldn't completely change her life or entirely escape from it. But through small, genuine actions, she felt a hint of freedom, like the first notes of a song she was just starting to learn.

One evening, after finishing a difficult task at work, Ramona felt restless and needed a break that her usual activities couldn't provide. Without overthinking, she took her bag and walked to the creek, a quiet place she had found recently. On her way, she stopped at a small kiosk and made a sudden choice-she bought a packet of fish food. This spontaneous decision brought her an unexpected comfort.

The path to the creek was lined with soft streetlights that glowed in amber, blending with the darkening sky. When she arrived at the creek, everything seemed to relax. A cool breeze gently hugged her, bringing the smell of damp earth and flowing water. She walked down the old stone steps to the water and found a place to sit. The creek felt magical—the full moon shone brightly, casting a silver path on the water, while countless stars sparkled above, their reflections dancing like tiny diamonds.

Ramona opened the small packet of fish food and sprinkled it into the water. Almost immediately, the calm surface came alive as fish swam quickly towards the food, their shiny bodies reflecting the moonlight. She watched them closely, her fascination growing with each graceful movement. Feeding these small creatures felt simple, but it brought out strong feelings in her.

She felt a wave of peace that surprised her. This feeling differed from her short satisfaction from completing a task or marking something off her list. It felt deeper like she had tapped into a calm inside her that she didn't know was there. Nourishing another life, even so small, gave her a quiet sense of fulfillment. It wasn't about significant actions or great successes. At this moment, surrounded by the serene beauty of the evening, she felt a clear sense of purpose—simple and honest.

Ramona sat quietly by the creek, enjoying the calm around her. For once, she didn't hear the demands of her job or the doubts in her mind. She felt a natural sense of peace. At this moment, with the fish swimming and the water shining under the moonlight, Ramona felt connected to something bigger. She didn't need to explain or hold onto it; being there felt right.

As she watched the playful fish, she suddenly heard her name called softly. The familiar voice stirred deep feelings inside her. It was someone she had missed, a voice that often came to her mind. At first, she thought it was just her imagination. But then she felt a gentle touch on her shoulder and heard the voice again. Her heart racing, she turned around.

There he was. Tom. He stood as if he had stepped out of a dream, the moment stretching beyond logic and time.

Ramona sat still for a moment, her heart racing. She was surprised to see Tom after such a long time. He stood tall and strong, his familiar boyish face still present. Though time had changed things, she remembered how much she admired him.

"Hi, Ramona! I didn't mean to bother you. I saw you sitting alone for a while and wanted to check—are you okay?" he asked gently, his voice unsure.

His concern surprised her, and she instinctively set up her defenses. "Everything's fine," she said quickly. Then she added, "I just... enjoying feeding the fish. It's peaceful."

Tom looked into her eyes momentarily, and something stirred between them in the moonlight—a connection she had almost forgotten. It was as if time had stood still, and they were back where they left off. She felt a strange thrill as they held each other's gaze, unsure what to say next.

"Feeding the fish, huh? That sounds nice. Maybe I'll try it someday," Tom said; his attempt to lighten the mood was palpable, relieving the tense atmosphere.

Ramona smiled and felt more relaxed. She reached for the small packet of fish feed beside her and handed it to him. "Here," she said gently, "give it a try. It feels good."

Tom took the packet from her. Their fingers brushed briefly. They sat side by side on the ledge, quietly tossing bits of feed into the water. The gentle ripples spread out before them as the night became still. Only the soft sound of the water and the quiet feeling of a connection between them remained.

It was the perfect setting to rekindle a love thought long lost. They felt a mutual sense of coming home, returning to a place they both knew well. The feeling was so powerful and undeniable that it challenged the narratives they had crafted to move on, to keep going forward without each other.

In that moment, time seemed to slow, and words felt unnecessary. They sat in profound silence, broken only by the occasional sigh as if both were trying to find a way through the unspoken. Perhaps, if fate had willed it, Cupid would have drawn his bow, pushing Tom past his hesitation to reach for Ramona's hand. And she, in turn, might have rested her head gently on his shoulder, allowing herself the comfort of closeness.

But nature had other plans. As if sensing the tension, the sky suddenly opened up. Rain poured down, breaking the moment. They ran in opposite directions without a second thought, their footsteps splashing on the wet pavement. What remained wasn't just silence—it was everything left unsaid.

As Ramona stepped into her home, she felt a wave of unexpected sweetness surround her. It was like being wrapped in a warm embrace. The air felt magical, and she wanted to hold onto that moment, like a unique perfume she could save for later.

But the rational part of her mind reminded her that it was fleeting, just a passing echo of the past that would soon fade. Despite those thoughts, she felt disconnected from them. She got lost in a more profound feeling that touched her heart and lifted her spirit, urging her to enjoy the beauty of the present.

Sitting at her desk, she opened her journal to make sense of the day. Usually, writing helped ground her, but it felt different now. Her hand hesitated over the page. After a long pause, she wrote just one line:

"I have worked hard to move on from this past affair. But now, why does fate bring us together again?"

She looked at her words and felt a heaviness in her chest. How many times had she thought she was over Tom? How often had she told herself he was just a memory tucked away? Yet, today felt like a sudden unraveling of all her defenses.

The rain outside clung to the windows, a reminder of that evening encounter. Ramona closed her journal as her thoughts returned to that brief moment—the silence, the unspoken words, and the rain that had washed it all away. Maybe it was nothing. Perhaps it was everything.

She took a deep breath, letting the thought linger. For now, she would sit with it, without answers, without clarity, just the calm that followed an unexpected reunion.

# FROM DARKNESS TO CLARITY

Ramona sat on the edge of her bed, her grip on the empty glass tightening as if it could anchor her in the present. The weight of the storm in her dream pressed heavily on her chest, and the sting of betrayal cut deep.

She shut her eyes, attempting to distinguish reality from the vivid, haunting images her mind had conjured. But the faces of her ex-lover and former best friend lingered—their once warm smiles now twisted, their laughter a cruel echo. It was more than a dream; it was a painful memory reshaped by her mind.

A chill ran through her, and she hugged herself. The room, though familiar, felt empty and too big. She glanced at the clock on her nightstand—it was 3:47 a.m. The silence around her was overwhelming.

Ramona set the glass down and got out of bed, her bare feet touching the cold wooden floor. Her thoughts were running wild, and she couldn't stay in bed. She went to the window and pulled the curtain back just enough to let the moonlight in.

Below her, the city lay vast and quiet, its lights stark against the darkness that filled her mind.

The betrayal, a painful incident from her past, happened years ago and was hidden behind walls she had carefully built. She believed she had moved on and created a new life. But the dream revealed how fragile her healing had been.

Her reflection looked back at her in the window—messy hair, hollow eyes, a woman worn down by unresolved pain. "Why now?" she whispered into the space. The words hung in the air with no answer.

Ramona pressed her forehead against the cool glass, still thinking about the sea from her dream. It called to her, showing her a vision of herself on the edge of a cliff, with wind whipping around her as waves crashed below. But something stopped her. Was it fear? Hope? Or just her strong will to survive, even though she felt broken?

"Not again," she said quietly, pressing her lips together. She wouldn't let the past take control of her—not this time.

She stepped away from the window and began to pace around the room, her hands trembling with unease. She needed to find a way to regain her sense of control. Her gaze fell on her journal, carelessly left abandoned on the desk. After a moment's hesitation, she opened it to a blank page.

The pen felt weighty in her grip, yet she pushed herself to write. The words flowed slowly, each one wrested from her inner turmoil.

I dreamt of the cliff again, and memories rushed back. I felt the sting of betrayal and a sharp pain in my heart. These strong emotions tried to pull me into darkness. But despite everything, I stay strong. I won't let them take over; I am still here, more challenging than ever.

Tears blurred her vision, but she kept writing, sharing her pain on the page. As time passed, a calm began to settle over her.

When she finally stopped writing, the room felt lighter. The betrayal remained, but it didn't hurt as much. Writing had softened the pain, giving her a moment of clarity.

She wiped her eyes and looked out the window. The city was waking up, with soft hints of dawn lighting the sky. Though it wasn't much, it felt like the first glimmer of hope—a new beginning on the horizon.

One day at a time," Ramona whispered to herself, the words wrapping around her like a comforting embrace. It wasn't a grand promise she made but rather a tiny, steadfast commitment to move forward. For now, that was more than enough.

As she returned to bed, her thoughts raced. She had tried hard to forget that part of her life and believed she had moved on. But was it gone? The losses she felt—relationships and dreams—had slipped away like sand, leaving her empty.

Moonlight filled the room with a soft glow, and in the quiet, Ramona realized she couldn't ignore her feelings anymore. The dream wasn't just about the past. It showed her present—her struggles with Tom, her worries at work, and the fears she had pushed aside.

She opened her journal again, her pen gliding more smoothly this time. Maybe I've been carrying the weight of the past all along. Perhaps I've viewed my separation from Tom through a lens of betrayal and anger. But sitting by the creek with him.

Her thoughts drifted back to that moment by the water—the quiet companionship, the moonlight dancing on the rippling surface, the fish darting beneath.

It was eye-opening. I've been clinging to the wrong perspective all along.

Ramona paused, a lightness spreading in her heart. That peaceful moment with Tom felt worlds apart from the nightmare of her memories. Where the dream carried echoes of loss, the creek held only stillness and quiet understanding. She wasn't that broken girl standing on the cliff anymore.

She wrote, " I thank God for this clarity, and I promise to let go of the past that no longer serves me."

Just then, her phone buzzed. She glanced at it, a message from Tom lighting up the screen.

"Good morning. Sitting by the water's edge and feeding the fish with you felt good and peaceful. I wish we could have more moments like that. It was lovely spending time with you."

A small smile crept onto her lips. She didn't overthink her response and simply sent back a smiley emoji.

Ramona closed her journal and placed her pen gently on its cover. The weight of her words felt less like a burden and more like a release.

Her phone buzz lingered in her ears, echoing Tom's message in her mind. His words were simple, yet they radiated warmth past her defenses. She hadn't realized how much she needed that connection—not just with him but with herself.

As she looked at her phone, her thumb hovered over the screen. A smiley emoji was not much, but it was enough for now. Tom was not asking for answers or promises; he offered her moments of peace, laying the groundwork for something new.

The room felt lighter as if the moonlight wrapped around her. Ramona leaned back and took one last look at the city.

Although the dream made her uneasy, it also helped her face the truth: the past did not have to control her. She was not stuck on that cliff or doomed to the crashing waves below.

Her fingers moved across her phone's screen again.

Good morning. It was peaceful, wasn't it? I'd like to do that again sometime.

She hit send and exhaled.

Ramona closed her eyes and relaxed. She felt steady for the first time in a long while, as if the ground beneath her was firm. She was ready to take the next step forward.

# STIRRING OLD WATERS

Bella walked into the room slowly, as if she was still waking up. She held a hot cup of coffee and enjoyed the strong smell. "Oh my God," she said with a tired laugh. "My brain is still in airplane mode." She rubbed her eyes to wake herself up.

Ramona looked up from her book and smiled. "How was your trip?" she asked, curious as always.

Bella sat in a chair and relaxed her shoulders. "This time, we worked with photographers to see the Northern Lights," she said excitedly. "It was amazing. We camped in a remote area, surrounded by snow and silence. The weather was harsh—freezing and windy—but the lights appeared..." Her voice trailed off as she remembered the beauty. "They looked like a living painting, with colors you can't imagine. Every night felt like a dream."

Ramona's eyes shone with excitement. "That sounds amazing—a real adventure!"

"Definitely," Bella said, her eyes shining with anticipation as she sipped her coffee. "And wait until you see the photos. We took so many, and I hope they turn out well." She leaned forward, excited. "And guess what? We're planning a cruise to Antarctica next! It's partly sponsored, so we hope to make it happen!"

Ramona laughed softly. "Good luck! You enjoy life," she teased, admiring Bella's adventurous spirit.

"Some trips are amazing," Bella said, her eyes drifting as she thought about her recent adventure. Then she smiled and said, "But enough about me. How have you been? How was the meditation camp? You look wonderful."

"Thank you for the compliment," Ramona said with a gentle smile. Her recent change made her feel bright and confident.

"It has been a truly eye-opening experience," Ramona said, her voice full of gratitude. "Thank you so much for suggesting it, Bella. I didn't expect it to change my life this much."

Bella leaned forward with a bright smile. "I'm thrilled to hear that. The camp helps people see things clearly, doesn't it? But what's going on with Tom? Did you meet him by the creek? And what about that dream you had—the one about the cliff? It seems like your past is pulling at you in many ways."

Ramona sighed and looked out the window, seeking answers. "Seeing Tom again brought back many old feelings—fears, doubts, and everything I thought I had buried. And that dream..." She paused, lowering her voice. "I'm standing on a cliff, torn between jumping or staying. Every choice has led me here, and I feel stuck. I can't shake the feeling that my past still controls everything." The influence of past relationships on our present choices is a fascinating aspect of human nature, isn't it?"

Bella's playful smile eased the tension. "Uh-oh! Does this mean my friend is leaving me for her long-lost love?"

Ramona laughed and shook her head. "Oh, come on, Bella. It's not like that."

Bella smiled but soon became serious. "You know," she said, "my teacher at the camp once mentioned something interesting. During our deep meditation sessions, people often find hidden truths about themselves. Our past affects us in ways we might not notice, guiding our choices, sometimes without our awareness. If we don't address those old hurts or unresolved feelings, they can act like instincts influencing us."

"That's exactly it," Ramona said, her eyes bright with understanding. "The meditation helped me see parts of my life that I didn't know existed. Now I understand how much my past has shaped me."

Bella hesitated and spoke softly. "I've been wondering something, and I hope it doesn't upset you." She took a moment to find the right words. "Why did Tom come back to you after so long? He's doing well with his music, and he's becoming famous. With all that success, a lot must be going on in his life. Still, he chose to return to you. Doesn't that mean something?"

Ramona laughed and rolled her eyes. "Oh, Bella, you're overthinking it."

Bella leaned back with a knowing grin. "Maybe, but we'll see how it plays out."

* * *

Ramona sat by the window, sunlight shining on her kitchen table. She held a warm mug of tea, steam rising into the air. Bella had left an hour ago, and her laughter still lingered in Ramona's mind. Now, with the quiet around her, Ramona found herself thinking about the memory of her dream.

The cliff always began the same way. She stood at the edge, watching the sky and sea stretch out endlessly in front of her. The wind tugged at her hair, whispering possibilities and threats alike. The waves crashed against the sharp rocks below, their loud sound mixing danger with attraction. She felt an urge from deep inside her, not from behind. It was a strange feeling that made her want to jump.

Ramona gripped her mug tightly. She had often woken from that dream, her heart racing and breathing quickly. When she woke up, she didn't fear; instead, she felt a confusing desire for understanding.

Her phone buzzed on the table, pulling her out of her thoughts. She looked at the screen. It was a message from Tom.

"Good morning, Ramona. I hope you're doing well. Would you have time for coffee this week? I have something I'd like to discuss."

She looked at the words, her heart racing. It was typical of Tom to be direct, even after all these years. He had a way of cutting through the distractions and getting to the point. But what was the point now? And why did he want to talk about it with her?

Ramona put down the phone. She wasn't ready to reply yet. Instead, she relaxed in her chair and let her thoughts drift. Bella's earlier words came back to her mind. "Our past shapes us in ways we don't even realize. They can feel like instincts guiding us until we face those old wounds or unresolved emotions."

The meditation camp had been eye-opening. It provided her with tools to understand her thoughts and to face her emotions instead of avoiding them. However, when it came to Tom, she felt off-balance, like the ground was shifting under her. Their relationship had always been a mystery to her; its end was not dramatic or explosive but a quiet fade, like a song losing its tune. They had moved on, or so she believed, but now he was back in her life, pulling threads she wasn't sure she wanted to unravel.

Ramona stood up and walked onto her small balcony. The cool air touched her cheeks, making her feel grounded. She closed her eyes and took a deep breath. At camp, she learned a method to calm her mind. She started this practice now, counting her breaths and noticing her heartbeat slow.

When she opened her eyes, she saw a beautiful horizon. The dawn colors captivated her momentarily, warming everything in a golden light.

In this quiet moment, she realized she had never seen what was beyond the cliff's edge in her recurring dream. She focused on the edge each time, torn between jumping into the unknown or staying safe in the familiar. But what if, she thought, something amazing waited just beyond that jump? A world of possibilities she had never imagined? This idea sparked a flicker of hope in her mind, mixing with the fresh air around her. What wonders or adventures could she find if she could step off the edge and face the uncertainty ahead?

*Her phone buzzed again. This time, it was Bella.*

*"Don't overthink it, Rami. Whatever he wants to talk about, you can handle it. Remember, you're not the same person you were before. Maybe that's why he wants to talk to you now."*

Ramona smiled slightly, thankful for Bella's perfect timing. She picked up her phone and typed a reply to Tom.

*"Sure. Let's meet for coffee. Just let me know when and where."*

She hit send before any doubts could creep in. A surprising sense of calm washed over her. It isn't just about taking a leap or staying put. It's about learning to stand at the edge and truly see what lies ahead.

# OLD SPARKS, NEW DISTANCE

It was a beautiful Saturday evening, and the city was coming to life. Ramona walked into the cozy cafe, excited and nervous about her coffee date. The smell of roasted coffee filled the air, mixing with the happy conversations of other customers and creating a friendly atmosphere.

There he was, sitting by the window, the sunlight highlighting his warm features. Tom looked up as she came closer and greeted her with a big smile that lit up his eyes. "Ramona!" he said, standing up to say hello.

"Tom," she said with a warm smile, her voice shaky.

They exchanged polite greetings, but their conversation included awkward pauses. The year apart had created a gap neither knew how to bridge. As they stirred their coffees, memories— some good, some painful—hung between them.

Tom tilted his head and looked at her for a moment. "You've changed," he said, sounding curious.

Ramona smiled slightly. "Time changes people," she said quietly, not looking at him.

Just as their conversation started to flow, a young woman in her twenties, full of energy, came to their table.

"Oh my god, Tom! I can't believe it's you!" she exclaimed, holding her phone. Her sudden appearance disrupted the delicate balance of their reunion.

Tom looked uneasy and glanced at Ramona. "Uh, hi... Yeah, it's me," he replied.

"I'm such a huge fan! Could I get a picture with you?"

Ramona raised an eyebrow and smirked slightly. "Fan?" she whispered. Tom looked at her apologetically as he stood. "Just a second."

Tom spent a long time taking selfies and answering fans' questions about his recent activities. Ramona sipped her coffee, feeling uncomfortable with their growing distance.

When Tom finally returned to their table, his energy lit up the small cafe. He had talked too long with people who recognized him, and their conversations drew the attention of others nearby.

Ramona felt many people watching her, and their staring made her uncomfortable and anxious. She needed a private moment to whisper with

Tom, but his charm and carefree nature drew everyone in, making her wish feel out of reach. This reunion wasn't at all what Ramona had hoped for. What she thought would be a calm exchange quickly turned into a public event, making the world around them feel like a stage.

She checked her watch. "I should get going," she said, her voice sharp, hiding her discomfort.

"Ramona, wait—" Tom said, reaching out as his voice cut through the chatter in the cafe.

But she was already getting up, quickly putting on her coat and scarf. "It was good to see you, Tom," she said, keeping her tone polite but firm to avoid more conversation. "Take care."

Tom watched Ramona leave the cafe. The door swung shut behind her with a soft chime. For a moment, he stood still, his hand reaching out to where she had just been. Then, he heaved a sigh and sank back into his chair, running his hand through his hair.

He replayed their recent conversation in his mind and the chatter that distracted him. Then frustration grew with every detail he couldn't change—the fan's interruption, the laughter, and the chatter that distracted him. Then there was Ramona. Her goodbye felt polite but distant, like a cold wall between them. It reminded him of his mistakes and left him feeling disappointed.

What did he expect? They could simply continue from where they left off despite everything. He had seen a flicker of hope in her eyes when she walked in, the same hope he briefly felt before the moment's weight pressed down on him.

Tom glanced around the cafe and noticed other patrons staring at him. Ramona looked different but still familiar. They had both changed. Sitting alone at the table with his coffee gone cold, he wondered if he had changed for the worse.

Outside, he caught a glimpse of her through the window. She pulled her coat tighter against the wind. For a moment, he thought about going after her, calling her name, explaining what? That he hadn't meant to lose this chance? That he still cared but didn't know how to show it?

Instead, he stayed in his chair, feeling hesitant. He watched as Ramona disappeared into the crowd, the city swallowing her.

Tom leaned back in his chair, his hands falling to his sides. Regret marked his face, sharp and unyielding. Despite all his words and charm, he knew he had failed to say the most important thing, the unspoken apology that carried the weight of regret and missed opportunities: "I'm sorry."

# AN OFFER TO CONSIDER

After meeting with Tom, Ramona felt a tightness in her chest. She had many questions, each needing her attention but offering no clear answers. These feelings were confusing and unsettling, but she was determined not to let them take over her. She took a deep breath and reminded herself that not all questions have quick answers and that some truths might remain hidden.

With this in mind, she focused on her work, which gave her a sense of stability amid the chaos in her life. The tasks before her needed her attention and helped her escape her racing thoughts.

Ramona began her morning by checking her email at her desk. She usually scanned the subject lines to find important messages. One email caught her attention. It was from Tanya, Mr. Sam's secretary, and that name immediately stood out to her.

Sam was not just a professional contact for Ramona. He was a partner at a vendor company she had worked with at her previous job. Their relationship went beyond professional. They had built a friendship based on warmth and respect, which is rare in her work.

Driven by curiosity, she opened the email. Tanya's message was direct, clearly relaying Sam's request to reconnect and suggesting a meeting. Ramona confidently reached for her phone and dialed the provided number without hesitation.

"Tanya speaking," answered a precise and professional voice.

"Hi, this is Ramona. I received an email about a meeting with Mr. Sam?"

"Yes, Ramona! Mr. Sam wanted to meet with you. Are you available for a meeting at our office later today?"

After exchanging greetings and discussing details, they agreed on a time for the meeting. As Ramona hung up, she felt excited. Meetings like this, which connect to the past, often lead to new opportunities.

She paused for a moment, thinking about her last talks with Sam. What did he want to talk about? She shook off her thoughts and focused on what she needed to do—getting ready for the meeting.

Later that day, Ramona entered Sam's office with a warm smile. The room looked elegant, with polished wood furniture, neatly arranged files, and a small plant in the corner. Sam stood up from behind his desk, and his broad grin lit up his face.

"Good evening, Sam! It's great to see you! How have you been?" Ramona greeted him warmly.

Sam is a man in his early fifties. He is charming, with a salt-and-pepper beard and a warm smile. His eyes shine with playful happiness as he waves to greet Ramona. "Oh, Ramona, it's great to see you this evening!" he says, his voice warm and friendly. "Thanks for coming on short notice; it makes my day to see you again.

Ramona laughed warmly, easing the atmosphere. "Hey, Sam! It's been too long, hasn't it?"

Sam relaxed in his chair, looking friendly. "I have to say, you've changed for the better," he said with a smile. "You look younger, fitter, and even prettier than when we last met."

Ramona laughed at Sam's unexpected compliment. "Oh, Sam, you still have your cheesy lines."

Sam pretended to be offended, then winked. "Cheesy? I'm hurt. I mean it, you know."

Before Ramona could reply, there was a knock at the door. Tanya came in, holding a tray with two cups of coffee. The coffee smelled rich and warm, filling the room with its aroma.

"Ah, perfect timing!" Sam said and clapped his hands. "Tanya, you're a lifesaver. But don't just stand there—come join us!" He waved her over to the seating area.

Tanya hesitated, her shyness evident. "Oh, no, sir. I don't want to interrupt."

"Don't worry," Sam said with a smile. "We're just catching up, and you're part of this team too. Please sit down. Ramona, you don't mind, do you?"

"Not at all," Ramona replied with a friendly smile.

"Tanya," Sam said, "you know Ramona. She's the best data analyst I've ever worked with. She played a key role in starting our company. Her advice boosted our sales."

Ramona smiled modestly. "Yes, the startup. I was very passionate about that project. I always liked the idea and am glad my work helped it succeed."

"It was more than just helpful—it made a big difference," Sam said, smiling.

Curious, Ramona asked, "How's the startup doing?"

"It's doing well and on the right track," Sam said thoughtfully. "But I wanted to catch up with you because the startup needs strong dedication to reach its full potential. I'm feeling stuck. My main business has become so complicated that I can't find the time the startup deserves."

Ramona nodded and listened as Sam continued.

"I tried to hire a manager to take over," Sam said, showing his frustration. "I was even willing to partner with someone who could help. But it didn't work out. I couldn't find anyone who shares my vision and drive." He paused, feeling the weight of disappointment. "I started this project with many dreams, and now... I hate the idea of selling it just because I can't give it what it needs anymore."

Ramona listened to him, sensing its emotional toll on him. "I understand, Sam," she said gently. It must be challenging, especially when building something important from scratch."

I wanted to discuss this with you. I hope you have some ideas or solutions.

Sam took a moment to find the right words. "I've been thinking... what if you joined the startup?" he suggested carefully. "I don't mean to offend—it's just a thought."

Ramona blinked, taken aback by the unexpected proposal. She didn't anticipate the conversation to take such a turn.

"Sam..." she said, her voice careful but interested. "Is that really what you want?"

Sam nodded earnestly. "I know it's a big request, but you understand this business well, Ramona. You also have the skills and vision to help it grow. I wouldn't trust this to anyone else."

Ramona felt the weight of his words. They stirred excitement, fear, and uncertainty she didn't expect. "I like your startup idea," she said, her voice steady but thoughtful as she considered his proposal. "I've always believed in its potential. But right now, it feels overwhelming. I need some time to think about it."

"Take your time to think about it," Sam said reassuringly, his understanding look making Ramona feel at ease. Feel free to take all the time you need. There's no pressure. Whatever you decide, we would love to have you on board when you're ready."

He pointed to Tanya, who was sitting quietly and listening to them. "Tanya has been with the startup from the beginning," Sam said with pride. She has kept everything running while I have focused on my other projects."

Tanya smiled and nodded warmly. "It's been quite a journey," she said humbly.

Sam leaned forward and said in a friendly tone, "Tanya knows the business well. If you have any questions or need help, she's the person to ask."

Ramona smiled back at Tanya, feeling relaxed by her calm and friendly manner. "I'll remember that," she replied quietly.

As the conversation paused, Sam stood up and offered his hand. "We'll be here whenever you're ready to talk more," he said with a nod. "Take your time, Ramona."

Ramona stood up and shook his hand. The brief touch felt warm and comforting. She looked at Tanya, who nodded at her. Tanya's small show of support helped Ramona feel more at ease.

"Thank you both," Ramona said, sounding grateful and determined. "I'll contact you soon."

She left the office with many thoughts at the end of the meeting. The cool evening air felt sharp and refreshing, a change from the warmth of Sam's office.

As she walked to her car, she felt the heavy weight of the conversation. It mixed excitement, uncertainty, and possibility. She understood that this was not just an offer; it was a chance to go back to a part of her life she once valued. The question was whether she was ready to take it on again.

# AT THE CROSSROADS

Ramona settled into her favorite chair on the balcony. This spot had seen her good times and hard times. The cool night air signaled a change in season, and the stars above shone brightly. She wrapped her arms around herself, happily enjoying a rare moment of peace. Thinking about that meeting made her smile. After months of hard work away from public attention, receiving recognition felt like a warm ray of sunshine breaking through the clouds. It made her feel genuinely valued for her efforts.

She took a deep breath, her breath visible in the cool air. The weight of the decision pressed down on her. "Oh Lord, why is this happening now when I'm finally happy freelancing?" she whispered, her voice barely heard over the quiet city below.

Freelancing had challenges, like irregular pay and unpredictable projects, but it offered her something valuable: freedom. She enjoyed the independence, creative control, and satisfaction of being her boss. The uncertainty didn't scare her; it became exciting. Most of the time, she was okay with the solitude that came with it.

However, Sam's offer stayed on her mind like an unanswered question. It wasn't just the chance he presented; it was Sam himself. He had a sincerity and authenticity that she always appreciated. The offer was interesting and stirred deep feelings within her. Her instincts told her to think it over, but she knew better than to rush a decision that could significantly change her life.

Ramona felt excited and grabbed her phone. She wanted to share this moment and hear another voice amid her strong feelings. Without overthinking, she called Rachael, her fingers shaking a little as she tapped the screen.

"Hey, Rachael! I need to tell you something," Ramona said, her voice full of excitement and energy.

"I knew it! Finally, progress with Tom, right?" Rachael said, her tone full of excitement and mischief.

Ramona's smile faded as she shook her head, even though Rachael couldn't see her. "It's not about Tom," she said quickly, her tone turning serious. "There's been no progress there since that meeting. Trust me on that."

"Oh," Rachael said, feeling disappointed and losing some of her excitement.

"Actually," Ramona said gently, "I got an offer today. Sam—my old colleague—wants me to join his startup."

"Wait, what?" Rachael's voice brightened, bubbling with genuine excitement. "That's amazing news!"

"Yes, it is..." Ramona paused, her excitement fading as she considered her decision. She took a deep breath; her thoughts conflicted. "On one hand, this opportunity could open new doors and help me grow. But on the other hand, I value my freelance work. It gives me freedom that I appreciate. Even if it isn't perfect, I have built a life that brings me joy and fulfillment."

"I understand," Rachael said, taking her time to think. "It seems like you find the offer interesting, but you're worried about losing what you've built. Returning to an office job might feel restrictive after enjoying the freedom of freelancing."

"Exactly," Ramona sighed, leaning back in her chair. The cool night air carried the scent of jasmine from the garden. "This is a big decision," she said, feeling uncertain. "I can't shake the feeling I'll leave something valuable behind." She gazed at the twinkling stars, each reminding her of the dreams ahead.

"Here's an idea," Rachael said after thinking momentarily. "Let's involve Jim in this. He is an auditor who is good at breaking down options and looking at things differently."

Ramona tilted her head and thought about the suggestion. "Jim? That's a good idea. He's logical, and I need that right now."

"Exactly," Rachael said with a smile. "Let's involve him. I'm sure he will help you sort it all out."

"Okay," Ramona replied, her smile returning. "Let's see what Jim thinks."

.Jim listened attentively, fully engaged, as Ramona opened up about the meeting, the offer, and her feelings regarding Sam. He could sense the importance of her words and wanted to provide her with the support she needed. When she finished speaking, he leaned back in his chair and crossed his arms.

"Okay," Jim said clearly. Please send me the startup's financial documents, including the accounts and projections. Also, find out as much as possible about the startup's and Sam's leading company's current situation. If you are seriously considering this, we must understand what we are getting into."

Ramona blinked, surprised by his request. "The accounts?" she asked. "What are you looking for?"

Jim smiled slightly, trying to be reassuring but still keeping some mystery. "I just want to be thorough. You might be surprised at what numbers can reveal about how well a business is doing or what the people running it intend."

Ramona trusted Jim completely, but she found his method unusual and a bit intimidating. She wondered what he could learn from a balance sheet she hadn't considered. However, she knew better than to doubt his ways. Jim always paid close attention to detail and checked everything multiple times. Trusting his process, she sent him every document she could get from Tanya and contacted industry connections. Over the next few days, she gathered information about the startup's progress and Sam's operations.

Despite trying to distract herself with work, Ramona couldn't shake off the unease that accompanied Sam's offer. It lingered in her mind, a persistent and unwelcome thought that intruded on her quiet moments.

*The opportunity was alluring, but it raised crucial questions. What would it mean for the life she had painstakingly built? Would it drag her back into a stressful cycle of deadlines, rules, and someone ease's goals? Or could it lead to something new—a chance for growth and a fulfilling adventure? The decision was not to be taken lightly, for it had the power to reshape her entire existence.*

The decision weighed heavily on her each day. It wasn't just a career choice; it was about the life she wanted. Freelancing had given her freedom and a chance to set her path, even if it wasn't always easy. Would joining Sam's venture mean giving up that freedom, or would it open up new opportunities she couldn't see yet?

As Ramona waited for Jim's analysis and collected more information, she realized something important: This decision would change her life in ways she couldn't yet understand.

# BEYOND THE COMFORT ZONE

One afternoon, Ramona sat at her desk, eyes fixed on her laptop, determination burning inside her. The numbers on the screen felt discouraging, but she wasn't giving up. The quiet of her room, usually a sanctuary, was now a prison, the distant sounds of the city a constant reminder of the world she was trying to escape.

Her phone buzzed on the desk. She looked and saw it was Jim calling. With a sigh, she answered, happy for the distraction. "Hey, Jim."

"Hi, Ramona! Can we talk now? I hope I'm not interrupting," Jim said calmly and reassuringly.

Ramona relaxed in her chair, feeling some tension leave her shoulders. "No, it's okay. I was waiting for your call. It's been a few days, and I must respond to Sam's offer."

There was a short pause on the other end. "About that," Jim said, sounding more serious. "I looked closely at the company's finances. It's in good shape—no major issues. I also talked to your dad for some legal advice. He said there aren't any big problems, just minor concerns about their main business."

Ramona frowned, surprised to hear her father mention it. "Dad? Why do you bring him up?"

Jim hesitated. "I wanted to make sure I considered everything. This offer is a big decision, and since you have a strong reputation in the industry, I thought it would be wise to get another opinion. Your dad knows a lot about legal issues."

Ramona tapped her fingers on the desk, feeling uneasy. "What's this really about, Jim?"

He cleared his throat. "This opportunity may offer a way to work outside of traditional jobs. Instead of joining Sam's team as an employee, it might be better to think about investing. This option could mean becoming a partner and owning part of the venture."

Ramona blinked as the surprising idea settled in. "A partner?" she asked, feeling shocked. She took a breath, her heart racing. "Jim, I haven't even thought about something like that."

"Absolutely," Jim said, his voice filled with urgency and understanding. "This is an important opportunity for you to grow and embrace a larger role. You have the experience, vision, and drive that make you truly capable. I know staying in a comfortable job can be tempting, but imagine what it would feel like to sit at the table. It would transform your future."

The words hung in the air, laden with significance. Ramona felt a constriction in her chest. She never expected to own and take on a role; the feeling was exciting and scary.

Her mind was a whirlwind of questions and uncertainties, but excitement emerged midst the chaos. Could Jim be right? Could she be more? She drew in a deep breath and spoke in a hushed tone. "I'm not sure, Jim. It's a lot to digest."

"I understand," he said softly. "But I believe in you, Ramona. I think you know you're ready for something bigger, too."

Jim smiled confidently. "Take your time. Don't overthink it—trust your instincts. Call me when you're ready. I'll talk to you soon."

As the call ended, silence filled the room, making Ramona feel heavy and worried. Many questions swirled in her mind, each more troubling than the last. Doubts filled her thoughts, adding to the uncertainty she couldn't escape.

She wondered why Sam would consider her a partner. How could I handle the finances for something like this? Ownership? That's for people who know what they're doing—people with experience, resources, and confidence.

*The idea felt strange and almost silly. Why was Jim suggesting something that seemed so beyond my abilities?*

*But then another thought came to mind, quiet but persistent: Or is it?*

Ramona took a deep breath and tried to calm her racing thoughts. She turned her attention to her laptop, which lit the room with a soft, flickering glow. She felt calm as she realized there was nothing urgent needing her focus.

She stood up from her chair and went to the kitchen. Making tea—filling the kettle, waiting for the water to boil, and steeping the leaves—helped her feel better. The cup's warmth in her hands helped her focus on the moment.

She took a slow sip and felt a strong urge to write. She went to the living room to get her journal. After flipping through pages of old thoughts and reflections, she began to write.

*The idea of ownership feels utterly foreign to me. It's like stepping into a world I don't belong in. I've never even considered it—do I even want this? The thought of it unsettles me like I'm being pushed out of my comfort zone.*

*Ownership comes with responsibility—financial risks, tough decisions, and leadership demands. It's a heavy burden to bear. Am I truly ready for it?*

*But Jim keeps saying I shouldn't underestimate myself. Could he be right? Could I do this?*

*Even if I wanted to, where would I find the money to invest? And what if I do propose this to Sam, and he says no—or worse, laughs at the idea?*

Is this what life is about, though? Taking chances? Pushing boundaries?

She put the pen down and closed the journal. Staring at the cover, she hoped it contained the answers she needed.

By late afternoon, she felt her thoughts were slightly more transparent but not ultimately settled. She picked up the phone and called Jim.

"Hey," she started, sounding unsure. "I've thought about what you said, and I'm... I don't know, Jim. The idea of owning something feels too far away. There are many unknowns and many things that could go wrong."

"I get it," Jim replied, his tone gentle. "Making such an important decision can be overwhelming, Ramona. Just remember, you won't have to tackle this challenge alone; I'll be here to back you up every step."

She heard papers rustling as he spoke. "We're taking a risk, but it's up to Sam now. If he's open to it, we can make this happen. Honestly, the required capital is not as scary as it seems. I've reviewed the numbers, and it's manageable."

Ramona's breath caught in her throat. "How will I present this partnership proposal to Sam? What if I mess it up? What if he doesn't take me seriously? The fear of failure is paralyzing."

"I understand," Jim said kindly. "It's tough to put yourself out there. If you want, I can come with you to the meeting. We can pitch this together. No matter what happens, we are doing this together."

His words were a lifeline, easing some of the tension coiled in her chest. "Thanks, Jim," she said softly, her voice filled with gratitude. "You've been such a great help. I don't know what I'd do without you. But I think I need a little more time to process everything before we move forward."

"Take all the time you need," Jim assured her. "It's normal to feel uncertain about something this big. And remember, we're family, Ramona. You don't have to figure it all out on your own."

A sense of cautious relief settled over her as she ended the call. The path ahead was still unclear, but knowing she wasn't alone made it less daunting.

# PATHS TO PARTNERSHIP

As Ramona strolled in the golden morning light, a stark contrast to her usual peaceful routine, her thoughts were unusually noisy and restless. The air was crisp, carrying a faint scent of damp earth, and the city was just beginning to stir in the distance. She cherished this time for solitude and reflection, but today, it was different.

She settled on her favorite bench by the lake, where she often came for clarity. She touched the wooden armrest and felt its worn grooves. The park was familiar but constantly changing—the sunlight made the water sparkle, a jogger ran past, and a couple chuckled on a nearby bench. Life kept moving forward.

She let her mind drift over the past few days—the conversation with Sam, the energy in Tanya's voice, the weight of the offer that had lingered like an unanswered question. And then there was Jim, his steady presence a quiet reminder that she wasn't alone in this.

She smiled as she thought about the feeling of belonging. It was very different from the solitude she had become used to—a life where she managed independently but often felt isolated rather than strong. Last night, Jim noticed the doubt in her voice. "I know you can do this," he said simply. His unwavering belief in her was both comforting and a quiet challenge. His trust was a powerful reminder that maybe it was time for her to believe in herself, too.

*She touched the edge of her Journal, A tangible reminder of her journey. She flipped through the pages and stopped when she saw an old entry. It was written quickly and angrily after her last day at her corporate job:*

*"This isn't the end. It's the beginning of something I haven't figured out yet."*

She exhaled slowly, the weight of that moment settling in. She vividly remembered that day—the ache of rejection, the uncertainty pressing down on her. She had felt lost. But looking back now, she saw something else: her independence. She had built something from nothing, turning uncertainty into a fortress of her own making. And now, she had the chance to make something even more significant—not just for herself but alongside people who believed in her.

Across the lake, a child tossed a pebble into the water, watching the ripples expand outward. Ramona followed the movement, watching how one small action set a pattern in motion. Maybe this decision was like that—a single step toward something more significant.

She closed the journal with a proud smile on her face. She had made her decision.

After much contemplation and soul-searching, She comes to a decision.

She was ready.

* * *

They scheduled the meeting to accommodate Jim. Ramona knew presenting the partnership proposal would be challenging because Sam was cautious and slow to accept new ideas. But with Jim by her side, she felt more confident and ready to handle any resistance they might face.

As Ramona and Jim entered Sam's office, they received a warm yet cautious welcome. Tanya's smile radiated friendliness, contrasting with Sam's gaze, which flickered with curiosity and perhaps a hint of suspicion at Jim's unexpected arrival.

Ramona confidently introduced Jim, recognizing the noticeable shift in the atmosphere as everyone focused on him. Sam, ever observant, did not miss the change either.

Instead of letting the tension build with unasked questions, Jim boldly approached to address the situation directly.

"Before we start, Sam, I want to show you something," Jim said, handing him a business card.

Sam's expression softened as he glanced at the name. "Oh, George! He's an old friend," he acknowledged, recalling their shared history.

Jim nodded thoughtfully. "Indeed, Ramona is George's elder daughter, and I have the pleasure of marrying his younger daughter."

Ramona saw Sam look back at her, surprised. "Ramona, you never told me that! Did you know Nancy, George's wife, is a distant relative of mine? We've always gotten along well."

Tanya leaned forward and said lightly, "It makes sense why you admire Ramona so much. It's a small world."

Ramona felt a change in the atmosphere. There was less tension, but something else took its place. Jim had used a good strategy by sharing a personal connection, which made it harder for Sam to dismiss her quickly. However, Ramona knew Sam did not let personal relationships influence his business decisions.

Jim redirected the conversation with a brief smile."George has always spoken highly of you,

Sam," he acknowledged, his tone showing genuine respect. "Leaving that aside, we believe there's a significant opportunity for collaboration. We would be thrilled to share our vision and walk you through the exciting possibilities we have in mind."

Ramona spoke confidently but openly. "Sam, Tanya, we admire what you've created. Your company has a solid base, and we see ways to help it grow. Our idea is straightforward: a partnership where we introduce new services, improve operations, and attract more clients without changing your current approach."

"We understand that growth brings challenges. We want to handle this in a way that benefits everyone. If you're willing, we'd like to schedule a follow-up discussion soon to go over the details and address any concerns," Ramona proposed, her tone indicating her eagerness for the next step.

Sam sat back in his chair, the wood creaking softly in the quiet room. He and Tanya shared a moment of silent understanding, a testament to their courage in facing the decision ahead. He didn't immediately accept her words but instead showed he was deeply considering the weight of the decision. Uncertainty flickered in his eyes as he pondered his options.

Tanya was the first to speak, her voice steady as she carefully chose her words. "We appreciate the effort and thought you put into this proposal. It represents a big change for us, and we will need time to think it over." She looked at Sam, who shared her thoughtful expression.

Ramona nodded thoughtfully, her expression reflecting understanding and unwavering determination. "Absolutely. Let's regroup in a few days. I'll prepare a comprehensive plan that outlines the potential risks, the benefits we could gain.

*Sam tapped his fingers on the polished desk, thinking about the proposal. "That seems fair," he said with a hint of satisfaction. With that, the meeting ended, and the atmosphere felt resolved.*

As Ramona and Jim left the office, she took a deep breath, feeling relieved but uncertain. "Jim, your support helped," she said, grateful.

Although the conversation didn't go as they wanted, it wasn't a complete rejection. They now had a next step, which felt encouraging.

Jim nodded, a small smile on his face. "You did well," he said, sounding proud.

Ramona smiled back, a hint of hope in her eyes. "Let's see what happens next."

* * *

In the following days, Ramona threw herself into her work, diligently refining the details of her proposal, which sparked her enthusiasm. Patience—something she often found challenging—felt like a heavy weight on her heart, but she recognized its significance on her journey.

Doubt continuously crept into her thoughts about the outcome. She replayed the meeting, reminding herself of what was at stake.

So, when Tanya's cheerful invitation to coffee appeared on her phone, Ramona felt an instant excitement. It lifted some of the burden from her mind, even if just for a little while.

*As she walked into the cafe, the smell of coffee and the soft music made her feel comfortable. Tanya was already by the window, smiling and friendly but unreadable.*

Ramona: "*This place is nice.* The coffee smell and the music are calming."

Tanya: "Yeah, it's a good atmosphere. So, how's work?"

Ramona paused, feeling there was more to the invitation. "It's... okay. Not great, but manageable.

Tanya thought for a moment. "We have been talking about your proposal. Let's set family ties aside for now. We trust your skills, so we wanted you here first."

Tanya stirred her coffee as she considered her following words.

"Ramona, I want to be straightforward with you. This company differs from the larger organizations you've worked for. We are a small team, which allows us to be flexible but also means we lack the safety nets that bigger firms provide. Every choice we make carries significant weight, and each mistake has immediate consequences."

She met Ramona's gaze, carefully assessing her reaction before moving on.

"Right now, we're dealing with tight budgets, stretched resources, and a steady client base—but not necessarily growing. We want to expand, but we're being careful. That's why Sam hesitated. Bringing in a new partner, especially someone with your background, is a big shift for us."

Tanya paused, carefully choosing her words. "I wonder if this change is big enough for you."

Ramona frowned slightly. "What do you mean?"

Tanya sighed. "You left a structured job and created something of your own. You're independent now, and I admire that. But if you join us, you'll be stepping into a company that is still growing. It won't be as polished, the challenges won't always be fun, and some days, it might feel like you've just swapped one set of frustrations for another."

She leaned back in her chair and looked at Ramona's face, trying to understand her feelings. "I just don't want you to feel like you're entering something too small for your skills," she said, her voice calm but showing concern.

Ramona furrowed her brow slightly in thought and nodded slowly. "Thank you for being honest, Tanya. I know that every new venture has its rewards and risks. But I believe it's worth the chance."

Tanya smiled softly, wanting to keep the conversation open. "Let's see what Sam thinks. He's at a function now, hoping to connect with George and Nancy. We'll catch up once he's back."

# BRIDGING TRUST

The meeting was over, but Ramona couldn't shake Tanya's words from her mind as she walked into her dimly lit apartment. She dropped her bag on the floor with a soft thud, took a deep breath, and headed to her small oak writing desk. There, her well-used journal waited, ready to hold her thoughts. With each pen stroke, she aimed to sort out the confusion inside her.

Tanya openly discussed the significant differences between this new venture and the strict corporate world Ramona had left. She discussed the exciting yet scary challenges of working in a smaller company—the lack of safety nets, the weight of every decision, and the unpredictable risks of investments. Tanya stressed the need to manage expectations, warning Ramona that this partnership might not develop according to her expectations.

Ramona tapped her pen on the blank page. Every choice feels important. Every mistake is noticeable right away. She kept thinking about Tanya's words.

As she gazed at the city lights, Ramona couldn't help but feel the uncertainty of her decision. She had left the security of a corporate job to pursue her venture. Now, she wondered if she was about to sacrifice her hard-earned freedom for a company still finding its footing.

She turned to a new page and started writing down her thoughts.

Advantages: Joining a growing organization presents an exciting opportunity for individuals to shape its development and success. Tanya and Sam's shared vision fosters a sense of partnership and common objectives. Furthermore, there is a significant opportunity to make a meaningful impact on the organization and the community, as fresh ideas can lead to positive transformations that inspire hope and optimism.

Disadvantages: On the other hand, we must consider the current financial instability, which challenges the organization's smooth operation and effective resource allocation. The organization's long-term future remains uncertain, raising concerns about its ability to withstand economic fluctuations.

Even though Tanya warned her, Ramona felt a quiet excitement inside. This was not just another job change but a chance to move toward something more splendid she could control. Having more control over her work and future was exciting and scary, but it also filled her with a sense of empowerment.

* * *

## The Wait

The next few days tested her patience. Her heart raced every time her phone buzzed, only to drop when it wasn't the call she had hoped for. The uncertainty was eating at her. Was she being considered, or was another name on a long list of candidates?

Finally, Sam called.

When she arrived at the office, Sam and Tanya greeted her with a warm welcome, and their hopeful expressions comforted her.

Had a delightful conversation with George and Nancy," Sam remarked with a satisfied smile. "Especially with Nancy—she holds an incredible affection for you. But as Tanya pointed out, we are pretty discerning regarding business. I'm sure you understand.

He pushed a pile of papers across the table.

"These are the terms for the proposed partnership. They are similar to what we created with our previous partners, but those plans did not go ahead."

Ramona confidently accepted the documents.

"Please take your time reviewing everything," Sam said. If you have any questions, please let us know."

That evening, Ramona promptly forwarded the documents to Jim.

After productive discussions with Jim and George, Ramona felt ready to proceed. However, she had one crucial question before making her decision.

* * *

## Conversation That Sealed It.

Ramona set up the meeting with Tanya at their usual cafe, which had hosted their earlier discussions. As she stepped inside, the rich aroma of freshly roasted coffee beans wrapped around her like a familiar embrace, filling her with comfort and anticipation. She spotted Tanya already seated at their usual corner table. Ramona slid into the seat across from Tanya and took a slow breath, savoring the moment before diving into the reason for their meeting.

Leaning forward, she traced the rim of her coffee cup with her fingers and asked, "What went wrong with that last deal? Why did it fall apart?"

Her voice was steady, but a quiet urgency lingered beneath the surface—an unspoken need to understand.

Tanya leaned back in her chair and sighed as she thought about their journey. "At first, we thought this partnership was perfect—there was enough funding and strong connections, so everything seemed to fit. But as we got more involved, we realized that money alone couldn't support us. We needed a partner who understood our industry and had insights beyond numbers."

Ramona nodded and listened closely.

Tanya continued, her voice calm and assured. "With your experience in this field and connections to people like George and Nancy, you make a perfect partner. More importantly, we believe our values and vision are in sync. That's why we think this risk is worthwhile."

Tanya's words resonate with a profound sense of certainty that was truly comforting.

Ramona felt confident about her updates, so she quickly took the revised documents from her bag and gave them to Tanya. "I made a few small changes based on our discussions. I hope this fits better with what we talked about."

Tanya accepted the documents with a warm smile. "Let's make this happen."

## The Decision

After a series of meetings and negotiations, they finalized the partnership.

Ramona signed the last document, realizing this wasn't just a new role but the future she was determined to build.

# A MILESTONE AND A MEMORY

A cozy, elegant office gathering welcomed Ramona as the company's new partner. The room buzzed with quiet excitement, filled with the soft clinking of glasses and friendly conversations. Ramona's family, including her supportive friend Bella, joined her to celebrate this important milestone in her career.

Sam clapped his hands together to draw everyone's attention. His voice rang with enthusiasm as he addressed the team.

"Good evening, everyone! Tonight, we come together to celebrate a new chapter for our company. I am happy to introduce Ms. Ramona as our new partner. She will be a great asset to us with her experience, insight, and dedication. Let's give her a warm welcome!"

The room filled with applause as everyone looked at Ramona. She stepped forward confidently, her smile bright but showing that she felt the moment's significance.

"Thank you, Sam, and thank you, everyone, for the warm welcome," she said, keeping her voice steady despite her mixed emotions. "I am honored to join this team and look forward to working with all of you."

The applause grew louder, filling the room with energy. Tanya introduced Ramona to important company members. Conversations flowed easily, and laughter filled the air as colleagues shared greetings and words of support, creating a supportive environment.

The event was in full swing when suddenly, the energy in the room shifted—subtle, yet impossible to ignore. Conversations faltered, laughter quieted, and an unspoken awareness rippled through the gathering. Ramona noticed the change but didn't immediately look. Instead, she felt it—the presence of someone familiar, someone significant. A slow tension curled in her stomach before she even turned her head.

Bella noticed it, too. She leaned in slightly and whispered,

"It's Tom."

He drew everyone's attention without speaking. His sharp gaze moved across the group and paused slightly longer when it met Ramona's.

A moment of recognition appeared on her face, but she skillfully concealed it, briefly tightening her grip on the stem of her glass.

Ramona took a quick breath, and her calm look almost broke momentarily. She forced herself to breathe out slowly, trying to control her feelings. Of all nights and all places, why did he have to be here now?

A mix of emotions hit her—surprise, a bit of warmth, and something more complicated that she couldn't identify. Seeing Tom standing there so quickly brought back memories she thought she had pushed aside. She didn't expect to see him tonight, especially not during such a critical moment in her career.

She reminded herself to stay calm as he approached with his familiar smile. She straightened her posture and controlled her expression. Tonight was not just any night; it was about her future and the success she had worked so hard to achieve. The weight of the situation was palpable in the air.

"Congratulations, Ramona!" he said with a warm smile, his voice as smooth as she remembered.

She hesitated briefly before smiling. "Tom, this is a surprise," she said, her voice betraying the unexpectedness of the situation.

He smiled, a spark in his eyes. "Jim and Rachael told me to come. They said I shouldn't miss such an important evening."

Ramona looked over at Jim and Rachael, who were talking nearby and seemed satisfied with themselves. That was typical of them.

She focused on Sam, who had been watching the scene with mild interest. "Sam, this is our good friend, Tom."

Sam's expression lit up with recognition, and his smile grew even more significant. "Oh, Tom! It's great to see you! Everyone knows you around here!"

After a brief but polite exchange, Ramona excused herself and approached her family, who were gathered in a cozy corner, eager to celebrate. The moment they spotted her, they rose with beaming smiles.

Rachael was the first to wrap her arms around Ramona in a warm hug. "Oh Ramona, that was so amazing!" she exclaimed, her face excitedly lit up.

Beside her, Jim nodded and said, "You did an impressive job up there. I'm so proud of what you achieved."

Ramona chuckled softly and shook her head. "Thank you, everyone. But honestly, this wouldn't have happened if you all hadn't kept encouraging me."

"Oh, come on, Ramona," Nancy said encouragingly. "You earned this. You don't need to hold back."

Just as Ramona was about to reply, a tiny, eager voice interrupted her.

"Congratulations, Ramona Aunt!"

She looked down and saw Lancy looking up at her, eyes shining with happiness. Ramona's heart melted as she knelt to her niece's level.

"Thank you, Lancy," she said, gently moving a curl behind Lancy's ear. "You look very pretty tonight!"

Lancy giggled and twirled happily, making her dress flutter. Just then, Bella joined the group with a playful look in her eyes.

"On the subject of compliments," Bella teased as she crossed her arms, "Tom mentioned he felt the same way about your speech."

Ramona smiled and raised an eyebrow playfully. "Oh? So, you've been making the rounds, huh? Did you get to meet my family and chat with Tom?"

Bella smiled and nudged her playfully. "For sure. And just to say, he looks good tonight."

Ramona groaned, shaking her head. "Bella, let's keep the focus here, please."

Bella smirked, but Jim tapped his glass before she could say anything else, bringing the conversation back to the celebration. The night continued with laughter, stories, and the warmth of friends and family.

Yet, despite her best efforts to remain present, Ramona found her mind wandering.

From across the room, Ramona watched Tom move through the crowd quickly—laughing, chatting, entirely at home. His deep laughter mixed with the buzz of conversation. He fit in naturally as if he had always been part of this world and no time had passed.

Curiosity tugged at her, strong and irresistible. Focus, she told herself, shifting her attention back to the warmth of her family. But the more she tried not to look his way, the more she felt his presence.

It wasn't just nostalgia. It was something more.

And then, as if he had heard her thoughts, Tom walked over, hands in his pockets, wearing that same easy smile she remembered.

"Looks like you've been busy tonight," he said lightly, though something was beneath his tone.

"Just... catching up," she shrugged. But no matter how casual she tried to be, she could feel her pulse quicken.

They engaged in small talk, the air thick with unspoken words and the weight of their shared history. Their conversation was light and polite, and they carefully avoided the one topic that truly mattered.

After a brief pause, Tom glanced around a hint of nostalgia in his eyes. "Feels like old times, doesn't it?"

Ramona hesitated, knowing he wasn't just talking about the party. He meant them—who they used to be.

"A little, I guess," she said carefully. "But things... they're different now."

Something flickered in his eyes—regret, understanding, or maybe both. "Yeah," he said softly. Then, with a slight chuckle, he added, "Funny how some things, or some people, keep crossing our paths."

Ramona let out a slow breath, feeling the weight of unspoken words between them. There was something familiar about him, a pull she wasn't sure she was ready to face. But before she could stop herself, the words slipped out.

"Maybe there's a reason," she murmured, almost more to herself than to him.

The moment lingered, filled with unspoken possibilities. But before either of them could speak, George walked up, giving Tom a friendly pat on the back and breaking the quiet tension.

"Heading out?" he asked Ramona with a warm smile.

She nodded, snapping back to the present. A wave of relief washed over her—but so did a hint of disappointment. As Tom stepped back, she said her goodbyes, sharing hugs and lingering smiles before heading out.

As she stepped into the crisp night air, laughter and celebration lingered in her ears, but her mind wouldn't settle.

She couldn't shake the feeling that this wouldn't be the last time their paths crossed.

And deep down, she wasn't sure if that thought scared her—or if she was hoping for it.

# STEPPING INTO THE ROLE

Ramona sat on her balcony, holding a warm mug of coffee. She sank into her chair, letting the sun's golden light wash over her. A gentle breeze, carrying the scent of fresh flowers, moved through the trees. Birds chirped, their songs blending with the quiet morning, drawing her into peaceful thoughts.

The memory of last night's celebration made her smile—finally, a partner. "Good going, Ramona," she whispered, raising her mug in a small toast to herself. It still felt unreal. Not long ago, a business partnership had seemed impossible—too big, too far from who she used to be. But now, here she was, a testament to her growth and resilience.

She took a deep breath, letting it all sink in.

It hadn't been easy—long nights, tough talks, and doubts that almost made her give up. But she had kept going, facing every challenge and proving stronger than she ever thought.

Freelancing had been her bridge—more than just a career move; it had given her the space to rebuild herself, to slow down, and to listen to what she needed. The meditation camp had been part of that—an experience that had shifted something deep within her, teaching her balance and grounding her in unexpected ways.

But even after all that, running into Tom last night had shaken her.

Some feelings just didn't fade so quickly.

She sighed quietly and set her empty mug on the table.

She had been pushing herself hard between finalizing the partnership and finishing her freelance work. The past few weeks were a blur of deadlines, meetings, and big decisions.

But now, in the calm of the morning, she finally let herself rest, feeling the stark contrast between the hectic past weeks and the peaceful present.

For the first time in a long while, no urgent task pulled at her attention.

She closed her eyes, breathing in the crisp morning air. It filled her lungs, melting away the last traces of tension. In the quiet, the world felt light and still.

This moment—this stillness—was a gift—a rare, precious luxury.

And she embraced it.

Because today wasn't just another day.

Today was the beginning of something new.

* * *

## A New Beginning

Ramona took a deep breath, steadying herself before stepping into the office. The rich aroma of freshly brewed coffee blended with the low hum of voices filled the space with a quiet buzz of energy. As she entered, the soft murmur of activity faded for a moment. Heads turned, eyes landing on her—curious at first, then warming with recognition. One by one, the team stood, smiles spreading as they welcomed her.

The team's quiet acknowledgment took her by surprise. There were no words, no grand gestures—just a subtle, genuine respect that filled the space. A flicker of vulnerability stirred within her, unexpected yet fleeting, quickly replaced by something steadier, something more substantial.

Back in the rhythm of office life—only this time, she wasn't just part of the team. She was leading it.

Tanya walked up with a warm smile. "Welcome, Ramona," she said, gesturing toward the glass-walled office at the far end. "Your space is ready."

Ramona took a steady breath, pushing down the emotions inside her. "Thank you, Tanya. You've always been a great help."

"Anything for you, Boss," Tanya said with a playful grin.

Ramona laughed. "Let's skip the 'Boss' thing, okay? We're a team. Just call me Ramona."

Tanya's smile grew, her admiration shining through. "That's why everyone's excited to have you here." She motioned around the room. "Come on, let me show you around."

As they walked, Ramona took in every detail. This was nothing like the big corporate world she had left behind. Gone were the endless rows of cubicles and rigid hierarchies. Here, the space felt open, alive with energy. Voices intertwined as conversations flowed naturally, ideas sparked and bounced from one person to another, and colleagues leaned in, fully engaged. It wasn't just an office but a place where collaboration thrived.

"We like to keep things flexible," Tanya said, nodding toward a lounge area with over sized chairs and a whiteboard covered in colorful sketches. "People brainstorm here, take breaks, or just talk things through. It keeps the energy flowing."

As they turned the corner, the energy in the office picked up. A young man was deep in conversation, gesturing wildly as if his words needed extra emphasis.

"And here's Jack," Tanya said with a smirk. "Great at his job, but..." She lowered her voice. "A bit of a handful."

Ramona raised an eyebrow, curious. Jack noticed them and flashed a playful salute, mischief in his eyes.

"Ah, the new boss! Welcome, welcome," he said with an exaggerated wave.

Ramona crossed her arms, a hint of amusement on her face. "Just Ramona," she corrected with a smile. "But I appreciate the enthusiasm."

Jack grinned. "Got it. Let me know if you need a pep talk—I'm an expert."

Tanya shook her head with a laugh. "See what I mean?"

Ramona smiled. She knew the type—driven, rebellious, and valuable beyond measure.

Every great team had a Jack.

She let the moment settle, absorbing the energy around her.

As she stood there, surrounded by the pulse of teamwork, the hum of ideas, and the raw potential of what lay ahead, she felt a profound shift in her perspective.

The uncertainty and weight of stepping into this significant role lingered beneath the surface, a palpable challenge.

Instead, it felt like a possibility.

She straightened her shoulders, a quiet resolve taking root.

"Alright," she said with a small, knowing smile. Let's get to work." Her acceptance of the new role was a formality and a testament to her growth and readiness for the challenges ahead.

# SEEDS OF CHANGE

Ramona became more comfortable in her new role and quickly learned the company's operations as time passed. She paid close attention to how things worked, asking questions and observing how different teams worked together. Her corporate jobs and freelancing background gave her a strong foundation, allowing her to quickly grasp project details, deadlines, and expectations.

Since she was already familiar with many of the company's major clients and vendors, she had an easier time building relationships and communicating effectively. Her friendly nature and quick learning helped her fit in easily, making the transition smooth for everyone.

Ramona's commitment to meditation and learning new skills changed how she approached work. She stayed calm and focused, making her interactions and project management smoother. Her colleagues admired her ability to handle tight deadlines without stress, creating a positive and supportive team environment.

Ramona's real test comes when a major client, one of the company's most significant, suddenly asks for last-minute changes to an important project just days before the deadline. The request makes the team rush, with everyone scrambling to make adjustments. Designers work late, deadlines tighten, and stress levels rise.

Before, Ramona might have felt frustrated or anxious, but now she responds differently. She takes a deep breath and momentarily steps back from the chaos, using the clarity she has gained from meditation. Instead of panicking, She calmly breaks the problem into smaller parts, identifying quick fixes and those that need further discussion.

In an urgent meeting with the client, Ramona stays calm, even as they voice their frustration with the current draft. Instead of getting defensive, she listens carefully, understanding their concerns without letting the pressure get to her. She suggests a clear plan: immediately fix the most critical issues and make further improvements after launch. Her calm and practical approach reassures the client and earns the respect of her team, who see her as a strong leader in challenging situations.

Later, Sam pulls her aside and nods with approval. "You handled the situation well without letting them take advantage of us. That's impressive."

Ramona smiled, taking in the moment. This change didn't happen overnight. It took months of practice—learning to stay calm, think before reacting, and adjust her mindset. The change wasn't just in how others saw her but in how she saw herself. She felt secure in her growth for the first time, no longer doubting if she belonged in this new chapter of her life.

Tanya especially reminded Ramona of Elle, a former colleague she had worked closely with for years before life took them separate ways. Tanya's energy and dependability brought back that sense of teamwork, making the workplace feel new and familiar.

Sam was also glad he chose Ramona as a partner. Her teamwork and strong project management skills balanced well with his and Tanya's strengths, making them a great team. While Sam and Tanya handled finances, clients, and operations, Ramona focused on schedules and keeping the team united. Together, they felt confident they could lead the company to success.

However, Ramona's arrival caused tension, especially among Jack and his group. Although they seemed professional on the surface, their actions created unease. Jack's team habitually took the best projects, left others out, and made the workplace feel exclusive.

Complaints about their behavior started rising, with more people discussing favoritism and entitlement. Jack and his team had a lot of influence as some of the longest-serving employees, receiving special perks and high salaries. They were even involved in hiring and big company decisions, strengthening their control over the firm.

The tension grew with rumors that Jack and his team ran a freelance business, possibly taking company clients for themselves. This worried employees and highlighted the dangers of relying too heavily on them.

Sam and Tanya, aware of the delicate balance, began exploring ways to reduce their dependency on Jack's team. Their vision for the company involved a collaborative environment where no single group could hold disproportionate power. However, taking strict action against Jack and his team was risky. Removing such influential employees could disrupt workflows, jeopardize client relationships, and undermine the company's market position.

They had to tolerate Jack's team without depending on them while preparing for the future. Meanwhile, Ramona's teamwork, problem-solving, and leadership quietly started to reduce Jack's team's influence.

As Ramona's influence grew, she helped create a more inclusive and energetic workplace, showing the change the company needed. To Sam and Tanya, she was a sign of hope for building a fairer and stronger future.

With Sam and Tanya's support, Ramona introduced brainstorming sessions with employees from all teams and backgrounds. These meetings weren't just for new ideas—they gave everyone, from junior staff to senior managers, a chance to share their thoughts. The goal was to promote open communication, reduce hierarchy, and encourage teamwork in decision-making.

The impact was significant. Employees felt motivated and appreciated as their ideas were heard by the management and included in plans. This involvement boosted morale and made everyone feel part of the company's vision. Teams worked together, combining fresh ideas from new hires with the experience of senior employees.

However, not everyone welcomed the changes. Jack, a senior manager with long-standing influence, and his team grew frustrated. They felt their power was shrinking as decisions were no longer theirs. To them, Ramona's ideas lessened their authority by giving equal importance to less experienced employees.

Jack's frustration spread to his team. They complained that the new system was messy and slow because too many people were involved in decisions. They started resisting quietly—skipping brainstorming sessions, ignoring ideas from junior staff, and subtly opposing Ramona in meetings.

Ramona felt the rising tension and knew she had a challenging task. She needed to keep the team engaged and inclusive while handling Jack's concerns. She wanted to acknowledge his contributions and help him understand the importance of shared leadership.

But Jack wasn't just resisting—he was paying close attention. Behind the scenes, he and his team tried to weaken Ramona's influence, quietly spreading doubt among essential colleagues. They made her ideas seem disruptive instead of helpful, questioning whether she was the right leader. It was a quiet but serious threat that could undo all her hard work, and she could feel it coming.

# BUILDING CONFIDENCE

The office buzzed with stress and relief as everyone processed Jack's resignation. It was the busiest time of the year, and deadlines were piling up fast. The team was already overwhelmed, and the pressure felt unbearable. Jack had often been absent and avoided teamwork, which frustrated his coworkers.

The breaking point came when Tanya, the firm and practical team leader, decided to fire an under performing employee that Jack had backed. Jack had long shielded the employee, known for being inefficient and complex. However, with the team overwhelmed by work, Tanya prioritized performance over loyalty. The decision shook the office—and Jack.

A few hours later, his resignation landed on the management's desk. It didn't just seem like a reaction—it felt like a statement. He claimed the company had overlooked his contributions, but for Tanya and Sam, his exit wasn't precisely a loss.

"Jack's been a ticking time bomb," Sam said during a late-night debrief, rubbing his temples.

"Always missing during crunch time, bad attitude—he wasn't a great role model."

Tanya sighed, folding her arms as she leaned back in her chair. "Agreed. His arrogance caused tension, even with his closest allies. Sure, there'll be some short-term disruption, but in the long run? It might bring some stability."

She hesitated before adding, "I won't deny Jack was among our most well-liked and longest-serving employees. His departure will shake things up; we'll probably feel it in operations for a while. But his behavior crossed a line, a risk we must take." She paused, then gave a small, knowing smile. "Besides, we can count on Ramona to keep things together."

Sam nodded, his expression warm with agreement. "Absolutely. Ramona's been the quiet pillar of this team. No matter what we've thrown her way, she's handled it with composure. I've no doubt she'll rise to this challenge, too."

Meanwhile, in the middle of it all, Ramona felt the weight of everyone's expectations. The sudden responsibility was overwhelming, but she didn't have the option to hesitate. She knew she had to step up.

She had seen the warning signs long before Jack resigned. His frequent absences and unwillingness to collaborate weren't one-time issues but a pattern that had only worsened. What unsettled Ramona most, however, was how her expanding role in office operations seemed to unsettle him. She noticed his discomfort and tried to approach it diplomatically, even suggesting to Tanya that he might need more time to adjust.

"He's been here so long," Ramona had said in one of their private talks. "Maybe it's hard for him to adjust to the changes."

Ramona had genuinely tried to connect with Jack to find common ground. But Jack only pulled away more—skipping important meetings, avoiding team discussions, and refusing to collaborate. No matter what she did, she couldn't reach him.

As she looked back on everything, a pang of regret crept in. Had there been a better way to handle things? Could she have done more?

"It's not your fault," Tanya reassured her when the topic arose. "We gave him every chance. Some people resist change, no matter how much support they get."

Tanya's words were meant to be comforting, but they didn't silence the questions in Ramona's mind. Still, one thing was clear—ready or not, the team was counting on her. And she wouldn't let them down.

As expected, Jack's resignation set off a chain reaction. A few loyal employees left, and a long-time client with strong ties to him decided to take their business elsewhere. Another client, though recognizing Jack's efficiency, chose to stay—a small but essential win during the chaos.

In the weeks that followed, the changes took a toll. The team struggled to adjust to staff shortages and shifting client relationships, stretching their resources thin. But amidst the chaos, there was a silver lining. Jack's former allies, who stayed, were more cooperative than expected. Without his divisive influence, they blended more easily with the rest of the team, and the workplace atmosphere slowly improved.

Even with the heavier workload and early challenges, the office felt lighter. The tension that once filled every meeting and discussion began to fade. Teamwork felt natural instead of forced for the first time in a long while.

Seeing the need for immediate support, Ramona turned to her freelancing network, bringing in a few contract hires to help with the workload. It was a risk, but it paid off. The new hires adapted quickly, bringing fresh energy to the team and easing the strain on existing employees. Their efficiency and willingness to contribute provided much-needed relief, helping restore balance.

The transition had challenges, but time proved they had made the right choices. As weeks turned into months, Tanya and Sam grew more confident in their direction. Bringing Ramona into their inner circle wasn't just a strategic move but a turning point.

Her steady presence reassured them that they were on the right path. More than that, she became a quiet source of strength, a reminder that they would face it together whatever lay ahead.

# CROSSROADS OF FULFILLMENT

Now more settled in her role as a partner and with work finally running smoothly, Ramona decided it was time to take a break and focus on her routine. Since the partnership began, self-care had taken a backseat, and she longed to reconnect with it.

"There is Nothing better than a free day and a solo morning walk," she murmured, sighing as the soft glow of the morning sun filtered through the trees. It is the perfect way to clear one's mind from the daily grind and recharge.

The steady rhythm of her footsteps on the winding path brought a sense of calm, and the fresh air filled her lungs with quiet renewal. After a short walk, she spotted a shaded bench off the trail. Sitting down, she let the stillness of the morning wrap around her like a warm embrace.

Ramona flipped open her journal, its worn cover proof of how important it had become to her. What once felt like an awkward habit now came as naturally as breathing. Journaling wasn't just a way to reflect—it had become a guide, helping her navigate the unknown.

Since joining the firm, her role has changed in ways she hadn't expected. She began to write:

*"My role has changed significantly since joining this company. I used to lose myself in the precision of data analysis, but now my focus has shifted. I enjoy guiding the team, recognizing their strengths, and helping them see their potential. It's not without challenges—some days, the weight of expectations feels overwhelming. But there's something deeply fulfilling about the process."*

She paused, tapping her pen against the page, then continued writing.

*"Take Raj, for example. When he first joined, he was hesitant and unsure of himself. I immediately recognized that uncertainty, reminding me of how I felt in my first big role. But with steady encouragement and feedback, I watched him grow. Just last week, he presented a project that impressed everyone. Seeing his confidence bloom was like watching a ripple turn into a wave. It reminded me why I took this leap into leadership."*

Ramona's pen hovered over the page as her thoughts drifted to Jack.

*"Jack's departure unsettles me more than I expected. Not because I'll miss working with him— but because he left with a certainty I don't have.*

*He knew what he wanted. And it forces me to ask myself, have I been playing it too safely?"*

She exhaled, feeling the weight of the question settle over her. It wasn't just lingering—it was growing, shifting something inside her.

Closing her journal, she let her fingers rest on the cover. Maybe she wasn't ready to face the answer yet. But she couldn't ignore it now. And that, she realized, was how every transformation began.

* * *

Bella arrived in the evening, expertly balancing two mugs of coffee in her hands. She handed one to Ramona before sinking onto the couch with a playful grin.

"Hey, busy bee! You're getting harder to catch these days," she teased, stretching her legs out. She smiled playfully. "Do I need to book an appointment just to see you?"

Ramona sighed long, cradling the warm mug between her palms. "Work has been insane lately, but I'm finally getting a handle on things."

Bella studied her intently, then gave a firm nod. "That's good. But speaking of pinning things down, I've been talking to Rachael and Nancy..." She paused for a beat, then met Ramona's eyes. "They think I should bring up Tom." Her tone was steady, leaving no room for avoidance. "And honestly? I agree."

Ramona raised an eyebrow. "Oh? What about Tom?"

Bella took a slow sip before setting her mug down. "They think I should find out what's on your mind. And honestly? I agree with them. Tom's a great guy, Ramona. You two just fit. You make a great team."

Ramona stared into her coffee, her expression softening. "I know he's a great person. I just..." She sighed. "I haven't had the time to even think about it. I feel like I've been in a bubble between work and everything else."

Bella leaned forward, her voice gentle but insistent. "I get it, Ramona. I do. But don't put this on the back burner forever. Sometimes, the things we think can wait can't. It's not about pressure, but time doesn't slow down for anyone."

Ramona exhaled, her gaze distant. "You're not wrong. And you know I value your opinion. I'll think about it seriously, Bella. I will."

Bella smiled, reaching out to squeeze Ramona's hand. "That's all I ask. Just don't forget—you deserve happiness. In every way."

* * *

"Bella's words lingered as Ramona sat in the quiet of her room, thoughts circling back to Tom... She found herself back at her desk, journal open before her.

## Journal Entry – Unfinished Thoughts

"Tom. I keep telling myself I'll think about it later, but later never comes, does it?"

She paused, memories flickering like old film reels.

- The quiet afternoon at the creek, tossing breadcrumbs to the fish.

- The coffee shop-where a fan's excitement stole the moment.

- The office party- where their eyes met across the room, saying everything words didn't.

"I wonder why our paths keep crossing. And every time, there's this undeniable, steady feeling like a thread pulling us back to something neither of us has fully let go of."

Her pen lingered over the page before she finally wrote:

"Maybe it's time I stop waiting for later."

She closed the journal.

This time, she doesn't push the thought away.

This time, she lets it stay.

# RISING TO THE OCCASION

The Worldwide Summit, a pivotal event, is fast approaching. Ramona is brimming with excitement at the myriad opportunities it offers. She cherishes the thrill of navigating the bustling hallways, meeting industry leaders, and staying abreast of the latest trends. However, a concern lingers in her mind—her company has not yet acknowledged the conference, potentially missing out on a significant opportunity.

It's time for her to take action and demonstrate the potential benefits ahead! This summit is not just another event; it's a tremendous opportunity to enhance their visibility and forge meaningful connections. With some courage and initiative, she believes they can truly stand out.

Ramona discussed it with Sam and Tanya during their next team meeting.

## Team Meeting

Ramona: "I've been thinking—how about we actively participate in the upcoming summit this year?"

*Tanya (raising an eyebrow):* "The summit? That's quite a leap. What's on your mind, Ramona?"

Ramona: "Our team is motivated, and our finances are strong. Now is the right time to explore new opportunities. Joining this summit could help us form new partnerships and collaborations. Even if we don't secure contracts immediately, the exposure and experience would greatly benefit our growth."

*Sam (nodding thoughtfully):* "Not a bad idea. It's certainly worth exploring. But we'll need to evaluate costs, logistics, and what we aim to achieve from it."

*Tanya (leaning forward, intrigued):* "Agreed. If we're doing this, we need a solid strategy. We should prepare a compelling presentation, a strong portfolio, polished marketing materials, and possibly product demos."

*Ramona: (enthusiastically)* "Exactly. If we position ourselves effectively, this could be a game-changer for us."

Their conversation quickly gained momentum as strong ideas emerged. Sam suggested effective strategies.

To Ramona, this was not just a suggestion; it was a chance to lead and guide the business down a new path by combining her past experiences with her aspirations.

And finally, a decision was made.

And now the hard work began. Ramona, Sam, and Tanya wasted no time forming a dedicated summit team—a highly curated group of marketers, strategists, and technological specialists. Their cohesiveness was evident, instilling a sense of community and shared purpose. Sam managed the company's branding, presenting a new and inventive image. The team's thorough preparation was evident, giving attendees peace of mind about their preparedness for the summit and reassurance in their abilities to handle any situation.

Amid the turmoil, Ramona felt a clear sense of purpose. She flourished in this environment, directing, organizing, and steering the team towards a common goal. The attendees believed they would succeed due to their commendable resolve.

As the summit approached, anticipation and anxiety filled the atmosphere. Tanya purchased tickets and confirmed their lodging arrangements.

Ramona gazed at the city skyline from her office window the night before they set off. It was a pivotal moment—not only for the company but also for her.

The team entered the grand, futuristic convention center, buzzing with excitement. Cutting-edge tech displays filled the space, with massive screens flashing welcome messages and booths showcasing the latest in AI, VR, and blockchain applications.

As they arrived at their booth, the team wasted no time getting to work. Sam adjusted a display panel while Tanya organized marketing materials. Just as they settled in, Sam's excitement was palpable as he pointed to the booth.

Ramona turned to look. When her eyes landed on her former employer's bold, familiar logo, unease coursed through her.

She hadn't anticipated this.

She felt a mix of emotions — nostalgia, discomfort, and pain from memories. She thought about the long nights spent chasing tight deadlines, the friendships built through shared challenges, and the bittersweet farewell that had brought her to this moment.

"I didn't even think about this possibility," she murmured, barely audible. "They're here... right next to us."

Sensing her tension, Sam placed a reassuring hand on her shoulder.

"I get it. Facing your past like this, realizing that you're now a competitor—it's a lot to take in."

Ramona exhaled slowly, nodding. "Yeah. It is."

Tanya offered a warm, encouraging smile. "Hey, you're not alone in this. We're here with you. And remember—you're not the same Ramona who walked away from that company. You're here because you belong."

Before Ramona could answer, a team member came over with a question.

"Ramona, can you look at this? We're choosing between two layouts for the display."

Happy for the change of focus, she studied the designs. After a moment, she pointed to one. "Let's choose this one. It's sleek and modern and shows our interactive demo well." The team member nodded and got to work. Ramona inhaled deeply, then squared her shoulders. The summit had officially begun.

Attendees were already networking, sharing ideas, and exploring new collaborations. Summit was more than just an event—it was an opportunity to establish her company's presence, reconnect with familiar faces, and impact the industry.

## A Familiar Face & A Promising Lead

As Ramona engaged with an interested visitor at the booth, she noticed a poised, high-profile woman approaching. Her sharp gaze lingered on Ramona before her lips curved into a knowing smile.

"If I'm not mistaken... is that Ramona?"

Ramona turned, immediately recognizing her. A potential client from her previous company—someone she had always admired.

She smiled and said, "Yes, it's me. It's been a long time."

The woman nodded thoughtfully. "It has. I remember working with you; it was always a learning experience."

Sam noticed the moment felt important, so he spoke up. "Yes, and now she's leading with us," he said, giving Ramona's business card to the woman.

The woman took the card, looked it over, and raised her eyebrows slightly.

"You're in charge now." The woman nodded and put the card into her bag. "I might need your team's help for my new project. You know how to reach me."

Ramona stayed calm and replied, "We would be happy to help. We'll contact you."

The woman smiled and said, "Great. I have some calls, but let's continue our conversation."

As she walked away, Sam admired Ramona. "That sounded good."

Ramona smiled confidently. "Let's make sure it is."

As the summit ended, the atmosphere in the room changed. It moved from busy talks to quieter discussions and goodbyes. Ramona took a moment to look around. She spotted Sam, who was engaged in conversation with an older man.

Her breath caught. She recognized the elderly gentleman instantly.

Her former boss.

She remembered a man who played a key role in her early career. He was a leader she respected, learned from, and sometimes found challenging. Feelings of nostalgia filled her as she recalled late-night brainstorming sessions, important client meetings, helpful advice, and moments of doubt he helped her overcome.

Steadying herself, she approached them, her posture poised but her heart unexpectedly unsteady.

"Good evening, sir," she greeted, her voice warm but measured.

The older man turned, his gaze settling on her with polite curiosity. "Good evening." His tone was neutral, his expression unreadable.

She hesitated for a beat before offering a small smile. "Sir, it's me—Ramona. I hope you remember me."

For a second, there was silence. Then—recognition flickered in the older man"s eyes, followed by something softer, almost paternal.

"Ah, Ramona!" His face lit up, his voice now rich with familiarity. "Of course, I remember. How could I not? You were one of the most driven young professionals I enjoyed mentoring. Where have you been all these years?"

Ramona opened her mouth to respond, but Sam quickly spoke up with a big smile. His voice showed his admiration.

"Sir, she's not just someone who's been here—she's now a partner in our company."

The older man looked surprised and happy. He chuckled softly and nodded as if this news made complete sense.

"I always knew you had tremendous potential, Ramona." His voice held the warmth of someone who had once seen the spark of talent in her and was now witnessing the talent fully realized. "It's truly gratifying to see how much you've grown."

A lump formed in Ramona's throat—not out of emotion, but out of the weight of this moment.

She had once sought his approval.

Now, she stood before him as an equal.

She looked him in the eye and spoke clearly. "Thank you, sir. Your words mean a lot to me. I learned a lot under your leadership—lessons that have stayed with me and shaped how I work today."

The older man nodded slowly, showing pride and thoughtful reflection. "It's rewarding to see former colleagues succeed and build their paths. Keep moving forward, Ramona. There are still greater heights for you to reach."

She exhaled, a small smile tugging at her lips. "I intend to, sir."

They shook hands—a gesture not of a former boss and an ex-employee but of two professionals acknowledging each other's journey.

As he turned to leave, Ramona stood still for a moment, absorbing the unexpected closure that had just unfolded.

She stepped into this summit, wanting to prove something to herself. Now, she walked away, knowing she had already succeeded.

# RECONNECTING AND REFLECTING

## Journal Entry

As the excitement of the international summit fades, I return to my daily routine. However, before the details fade, I want to express what this experience meant.

The summit was an exciting event filled with energy, ideas, and hopes. I recognized familiar faces and met new people. Conversations sparked new ideas, and I felt connected to my career's past, present, and future. Seeing former colleagues, mentors, and peers succeed made me proud and a bit nostalgic. We started on the same journey, facing challenges together, but we have taken different paths. Each of us has built our place in the industry.

One moment stood out during my reflection: a genuine compliment from my former boss. His words were kind and meaningful. He reminded me of my early days in the industry when I started as a new graduate. I was eager but unsure, learning from his guidance. Years later, hearing him recognize my growth and the person I have become felt important.

The summit was more than just a career achievement. It showed change, resilience, and the crucial effects of my choices. It reminded me that even if our paths differ, the core of our journey—our connections, growth, and lessons—shapes who we are. Perhaps that is the most valuable lesson of all.

* * *

## Back at Work

Ramona stood outside the office building, thinking about the summit. The past few days had been full of new ideas, re connections, and some quiet insights. As she faced her usual routine, she took a deep breath to focus on the present.

*It's time to move forward.*

She squared her shoulders and pushed open the door. The familiar sound of the office welcomed her, and she quickly moved from thinking to doing.

Under her guidance, the team swiftly moved forward, following up with summit visitors, nurturing leads, and preparing to negotiate with a high-profile client from her former company. Ramona found it ironic that she was now competing against the organization that had once helped her career. This was a crucial moment that tested her determination and her ability to balance professionalism with ambition.

With strong support from Sam and Tanya, Ramona led her team through tough negotiations and high-pressure meetings. Sam, known for his analytical skills, played an essential role in shaping their strategy. He carefully analyzed data, predicted objections, and adjusted their pitch to meet the client's changing needs. When Ramona's former company made a counteroffer, using their long relationship with the client, Sam's strategic insight helped them create a strong value proposition that competed and stood out. His ability to stay calm under pressure gave the team the confidence to move forward.

Tanya focused on building a strong relationship with the client. She followed up consistently, making sure each interaction showed credibility and value. When a key decision-maker hesitated, possibly due to loyalty to Ramona's former company, Tanya reassured them with warmth and persuasive communication. She skillfully guided the conversation back in their favor. Tanya could sense and address unspoken concerns before they become problems.

Ramona, Sam, and Tanya worked well together. Ramona set the vision, Sam planned the strategy, and Tanya built the critical human connections that made their deals more than just transactions. They spent late nights and early mornings refining proposals, analyzing market positions, and solving unexpected problems. The pressure was high, but so was their determination.

After weeks of hard work, the team achieved a significant milestone: They secured a contract with a high-profile client. This victory was important because they had redirected the client from Ramona's former company, which added extra validation to their efforts.

The office was lively, and the team felt proud as they celebrated their hard work. This success was not just about the numbers; it showed their teamwork, adaptability, and belief in overcoming challenges. For Ramona, it was another reminder that good leadership inspires others to push their limits and explore new possibilities.

* * *

## The Celebration

Ramona and her team celebrated their achievement by taking a break from deadlines and meetings for a digital detox picnic. Free from technological distractions, they relaxed, recharged, and connected while enjoying nature.

Their destination was a serene lakeside haven on the city's outskirts, renowned for its pristine waters and lush greenery. They arrived early in the morning, welcomed by the golden sunrise and a fresh breeze carrying the scent of pine and earth. The air itself felt different—lighter, freer, and unburdened by the weight of deadlines and schedules.

As the day passed, the team quickly settled into a mood of fun and relaxation. Some people took over the barbecue, marinating meats and vegetables before grilling them nicely over open flames. Soon, the lakeside smelled delicious with the rich, smoky aroma of sizzling food, making everyone eager to eat. Laughter filled the air as colleagues discussed the best ways to cook the corn on the cob and season the skewers.

Others gravitated toward music and dance, transforming the clearing into an impromptu festival. Someone produced a Bluetooth speaker— one of the few modern indulgences they allowed— and soon, melodies flowed through the space. A spontaneous dance circle formed, feet tapping against the soft grass as people lost themselves in the rhythm, inhibitions melting away in the golden afternoon light.

For the more thoughtful members of the group, storytelling became an important activity. They gathered under the shade of tall trees and shared stories that mixed feelings of nostalgia, humor, and imagination. Some shared funny office mistakes that looked amusing in hindsight. Others shared personal stories that strengthened their connections in a way that no team-building exercise could.

Some people found peace while fishing at the edge of the water. They enjoyed the simple act of casting lines into the lake, which helped them relax. Ramona, Sam, and Tanya, who often led the team in high-pressure projects, took a break to laugh at inside jokes, skip stones across the water, and enjoy the calm surroundings.

This break wasn't just a celebration of their success but a re calibration, a chance to rediscover life beyond work. Their relationship changed as they laughed, danced, cooked, and shared stories. They were no longer just colleagues; they had become a close-knit group connected by experiences beyond work tasks and deadlines.

As they finished packing, the sky was a beautiful mix of orange, pink, and blue, reflecting the calm lake. They departed with one last glance at the serene landscape, carrying the day's warmth with them. When they returned to the city, their spirits felt lighter, their connections deeper, and their resolve stronger.

# HOMECOMING OF THE HEART

George and Nancy planned a family gathering that everyone had looked forward to—the event aimed to bring everyone closer together. Ramona, wanting to feel at home, returned to her hometown for the gathering. Bella agreed to go with her after Nancy and Rachael encouraged her.

When Ramona returned to her hometown, she felt a strong wave of nostalgia. Familiar sights and sounds filled her with happiness, and being with her family gave her a deep sense of belonging and joy. She cherished every moment of the reunion.

Ramona was pleasantly surprised to see Lancy, who had grown so much since their last meeting. Lancy's innocent smile and warm hug melted Ramona's heart, and her gentle gestures spoke of a child filled with love and curiosity. Hearing that Lancy had started going to school brought a glow of pride to Ramona's face.

Rachael, too, seemed to be thriving. She had recently returned to her teaching career, a step that had reignited a sense of purpose and fulfillment in her.

As evening settled in, Ramona stepped onto the porch, embracing the cool air around her. In the gentle glow of twilight, the familiar streets of her childhood came into view, stirring a deep sense of belonging. This visit reassured her that home would always be a part of her no matter how far she traveled. With a contented sigh, she turned back toward the house, drawn to the warmth of her family inside.

By nightfall, the family had arrived at the gathering. George and Nancy had worked hard to plan a beautiful, intimate celebration with close friends and family. Soft music played in the background while laughter and cheerful conversations filled the air, creating a warm and welcoming atmosphere. This event was more than just a party; it celebrated their shared connections and the special moments that made the home feel important.

Rachael and Bella exchanged sneaky smiles during the fun celebration and took Ramona's arm. Their smiles made people curious.

"Come with us," Rachael whispered, leading her away from the lively crowd toward a quieter corner of the hall.

The soft glow of the fairy lights filled the quiet space, creating a cozy feeling. Ramona's breath caught when she saw Tom standing under the lights. A mix of emotions overwhelmed her—happiness, surprise, love, and the realization that she had been waiting for this moment without knowing it.

Tom took a deep breath and dropped to one knee. With intense dedication, his eyes looked directly into hers. He held a shining ring in his hand that reflected the promise he was about to make.

"Ramona," he said, his voice calm even though he felt strong emotions, "you have brought so much joy into my life. Will you marry me and be my partner forever?"

For a moment, everything was quiet. The sounds around Ramona faded away, leaving only her fast-beating heart and the moment's weight. Tears glistened as she looked at the man she loved, who had always been patient, kind, and supportive.

There was a time when she questioned happiness. Love felt weak, slipping away whenever she tried to hold onto it. But life surprised her. It tested her, hurt her, and ultimately helped her grow stronger.

She stood under the warm glow of fairy lights with the man who taught her that love isn't about big gestures or perfect moments. Love is about staying, choosing, and believing.

Her voice shook, not from fear, but from confidence. A single tear ran down her cheek, not from sadness but from healing.

**"Yes, Tom," she whispered, her lips curling into a smile. "Yes, I'll marry you."**

Cheers filled the room as family and friends gathered to see the proposal. They came out from the shadows, clapping and laughing. George and Nancy congratulated the newly engaged couple. It was the perfect ending to an unforgettable day—a moment where love was the focus.

*"Ramona's journey of discovering herself, being strong, and finding love reached an important point. A new chapter is coming, but this moment is hers to enjoy.*